JARED

Boyfriend For Hire, Book 4

RJ SCOTT
MEREDITH RUSSELL

Love Lane Books

Jared, Boyfriend for Hire, Book 4

Copyright © 2021 by RJ Scott

Copyright © 2021 by Meredith Russell

Cover design by Meredith Russell

Edited by Sue Laybourn

ISBN: 9781785645426

RJ ~ Always for my family.

Meredith ~ For my family and friends for their continued love and support. And thank you to RJ for allowing me to create another beautiful story with her.

Boyfriend for Hire
JARED

RJ SCOTT & MEREDITH RUSSELL

Love Lane Books

Chapter One

Gideon tapped the paperwork on his desk with a very expensive-looking pen. "I'm just playing devil's advocate here, but do you think maybe you should have considered the consequences before you acted?"

Jared's chest tightened because sitting in Gideon's office at Bryant & Waites reminded him of sitting in the principal's office. He felt as if a ton of trouble was heading his way, and it didn't help that Gideon was stony-faced.

"I didn't know it was going to happen," Jared defended himself.

"But you had to know it *might* happen."

Jared didn't have a comeback for that at all.

Gideon sighed heavily. "Exactly who do you think will be covering the repair bill?" he asked with absolute calm.

Jared had seen the amount the hotel was asking for, it was the wrong side of two thousand dollars, and even though he'd known that question was coming, he winced. He hadn't expected the ex-husband of his booked date would cause *that* much damage to a hotel room, but Gideon was right—maybe he *should* have thought about it more. He'd been aware of the volatile back story between the ex and the man who'd hired Jared, hence the need to approach Bryant & Waites in the first place, but Jared had never imagined in his wildest dreams he'd be in the middle of a marital feud. Let alone see so much chaos done by one man in a hotel room.

"He looked so sad."

Gideon raised a single eyebrow. "I'm sorry?"

Shit. "The ex-husband—Bill, his name is Bill—well, he looked sad. He came to the door and when he explained how much he loved Yan, that's the name of the guy who hired me."

"I know who Yan is, Jared."

"Well, I thought Bill was going to cry."

"So, let's get this clear. You get hired to be Yan's date who explicitly said his ex was an asshole. Said ex then cries and you, in your infinite wisdom, let him into the suite that *we* paid for. The same suite for which we're now on the hook to cover damages?"

"It's just… I couldn't leave a crying man out in the corridor. That wouldn't be right, and I thought about the company policy of caring." Jared hoped that would vindicate him, but a nerve twitched next to Gideon's right eye.

"Company policy is to look after the client."

"I could see in Bill's expression that he was missing

Yan, and Yan said some things that made me think that he actually loved his ex, and that—"

"And then what happened?" Gideon interrupted.

"Well, then I went down to find Yan, who was waiting for me at dinner—"

"And you left Yan's ex-husband in the suite. On his own."

"I thought it was for the best. I'm sorry and I hope we're insured?" Jared hoped that was true because he couldn't cover the cost. God, the thought that he might have to find money for a broken television, not to mention the bedclothes shredded on the floor, made him come out in hives. He was only just covering rent and costs for his course, and he had the typical issues of any twenty-eight-year-old late to education where it was a struggle to make ends meet. He'd fucked up a few too many times and he could feel it in his bones that he was on the edge of not being put forward for jobs, or maybe being fired outright.

"That's not the point Jared, it's just one thing after another, not to mention the other issues marked in your file," Gideon continued.

"Which issues?" Jared couldn't recall anything in the last couple of months. There again he hadn't seen Gideon since Christmas because Rowan had dealt with the last booking. He didn't have to be studying psychology to see that Gideon was tense and wondering how to word what he wanted to say. Stress caused Gideon to hunch his shoulders, and Jared felt guilty for what he'd managed to do, but surely Gideon would weigh the problems against the repeat business that Jared had brought in over the past three years. He was good at his job, and he had to remember that and persuade Gideon not to fire him.

He didn't want to leave.

"New Year and the emergency exit call you made to Rowan to get away from a foursome for a start."

Oh, *that* issue. "It wasn't exactly a foursome. We all had our clothes on, and one of the men was all upset about his dog, and he cried, and… it was just a big misunderstanding."

"Jared," he opened a file on his desk. "One missing advent swan, a narrowly avoided foursome, a destroyed room, and that's in less than three months. If it wasn't for the positive feedback and the fact that all three of those bookings gave you glowing reviews, *despite* the issues—"

"Am I fired? I'm sorry, I didn't know that the swan belonged to the hotel, otherwise when the girl from the table next to me started sobbing I wouldn't have gotten involved and opened the gate to let it out."

"No, you're not fired, but Jared, you have to stop trying to make everything better for everyone and open us up to situations that cost money or reputation. So, this next booking…"

"Is my last chance?" Jared finished and remained hopeful that Gideon wasn't going to get rid of him.

"End of May we've just booked a graduation event for one of our new clients, she's a CEO and won't take any drama, tell me I'm not going to get a report that any shit has hit any one of the fans in any room you are in."

Jared held up a hand. "I solemnly swear."

Gideon muttered something under his breath and then pressed the intercom. "Rowan, can you bring in the ZenTech Industries file?" There was static, and Gideon frowned at the machine as if it had personally hurt him. "Rowan?"

Just as Gideon stood to find his errant PA, Rowan's voice came through loud and clear. "I'd love to come in, babe…sir, but we have a slight issue."

"What kind of issue?"

Despite the ominous mention of an issue, Jared watched Gideon smile at the sound of Rowan's voice, and how it softened his stern expression—that made it seem less probable that Gideon was going to kill Jared with his stare. It hadn't taken long for the grapevine to supply the juicy details that Gideon had realized his feelings for Rowan and had spent an *interesting* Christmas break in Maine. Fifteen months later and they had the same loved-up glow even now, although they attempted to keep things professional around clients, the guys who worked for Gideon could see the change. He was softer, happier, and his hard edges had been smoothed away.

I want that. I want a man who will rub on my hard edges. Jared bit his lip to stop laughing out loud at the thought, and instead assumed the pose of someone who was *absolutely* a complete professional.

"I think you might want to come out here," Rowan offered, and Gideon left the room. Unable to do much else, Jared went to the window, looking down at the people hurrying past on Stuyvesant Street, clearly on a mission to go somewhere, along with the tourist types taking photos of the brownstones. The offices of Bryant

& Waites were discreet, with a simple brass plaque explaining who they were, but nothing about what they did. The New York day was March-chilled, with blue skies and everyone still bundled up in coats, but spring was promised along with looming exam deadlines.

After this year he had one more semester, and then he was done with the first part of his education, his degree in psychology assured—as long as he didn't fuck that up as much as he kept messing up his bookings with Bryant & Waites. At least he was *good* at psychology and it had taken him years to save up to start his degree, a succession of shitty jobs building his pot of money as he lived in his parents' basement. Now he was nearing the end of stage one in his career, and ready to move onto his work placements.

"Okay where were we?" Gideon came back into the room, took a seat, and ruffled files, which was Jared's cue to sit down again.

"Is everything okay?"

"Rowan is dealing with it."

"You agreed you weren't going to fire me," Jared reminded him, hoping to get Gideon to crack a smile, but all he did was frown. *Not going well.*

"No firing. Not today anyway. So, the CEO of ZenTech Industry is a woman called Elisa…"

The rest of the short meeting blurred into details and dates, and by the time Jared left he had a new booking firmly fixed after his exams, which meant he had time to study and get his head straight. No more messing up bookings, no more swans, or ex-husbands, or unforeseen foursomes. When he got out to reception

Rowan was standing at the front door staring at something beyond.

"I didn't get fired," Jared announced with pride, but Rowan just huffed and didn't move from the door. "What's up?"

"There's a kid on our steps," Rowan muttered, "and he said his dad was coming but that was ten minutes ago and no sign of the dad." He shrugged into his coat. "I'm going to get him in and call the cops—a kid that age shouldn't be on his own. Poor boy is all upset about his dad, and something about his mom. He came in trying to hire a boyfriend."

"For real?"

"This is ridiculous, Gideon said to watch him and wait for the dad, but it's not sitting right with me. I've tried to bring the kid inside, but the last time I asked he refused to move. I'm going to sit there with him."

"You want me to talk to him?" Jared didn't know where that came from, but he could see Rowan was upset and worried, and Jared had slipped easily into his super-helpful mode without even realizing.

"You're sure?"

"I'm on it."

"Good luck, shout if you need me."

Jared zipped his coat and headed out.

Three steps down and he drew level with the kid. "Hey," he murmured so as not to scare him.

The boy glanced up at him, around ten or so, dark hair sticking out from a beanie, wearing a thick green coat, jeans, and Nikes. He hugged a dark notebook and was on the verge of tears.

My kryptonite.

The boy gave him a tremulous smile. "Hi."

"What ya doin', buddy?"

"Sitting."

Jared considered what to do next, and none of the options included walking off and leaving the kid. At least the March snows had melted away, and the boy wouldn't be freezing, but still, he was alone.

"What's your name?"

"Luka."

"Hey, Luka, I'm Jared." He offered a fist to bump, and Luka didn't leave him hanging, his notebook slipping. He caught it and then stared back up at Jared.

"Do you work in there?" he asked.

Jared caught the glint of interest in dark eyes. "Yes. Do you work around here too?"

"I'm only eleven," he scoffed.

"How about school then?"

"It finished at three."

"And you thought sitting on a step in the cold was a good idea to pass the time."

"I'm not cold." He shivered a little and exposed the lie for what it was.

"Where are your folks?" Jared wondered if Rowan was right and they should take Luka into the office, or just go straight to calling the cops, because there was no way he or Rowan were leaving him sitting here.

"Dad's at work but I had to come here and see you."

"Me?" Jared couldn't recall having met the kid, but there was no doubting Luka's conviction.

"Not just you, all of you. My dad works a lot,

running the bar, and he's always looking after me, or working, and since my mom died…" He cleared his throat, the words difficult to say. Compassion flooded Jared and he edged a little closer to Luka, offering non-verbal support where he could. "I want him to have a friend, and I want him to go on a date, and it doesn't matter if it's a girl or boy, because my Auntie Lee says he's bri-sextual."

Bri-sextual? Jared folded his arms and leaned against the stair railing.

"So, I came here to get one for him, but they said that my dad would need to go in, and they wanted me to stay so they could call the cops. But I don't need to be arrested. Plus, that man, he gave me a card, said Dad could call the number on it if he wanted, but I can't tell Dad he needs to go in to get a friend, 'cause he'd kill me, not for real, but he'd be angry, and now I don't know what to do."

"Do you have your dad's number?"

"No," Luka said, but wouldn't meet his eyes.

Jared read Luka's lie—this kid was transparent. "Is there someone waiting at home for you? What's your address?"

"I forget. Look, can I read you something?" Luka asked with a tinge of hope in his voice.

"Once you give me your address, then sure."

"How about I read this and *then* give you my address."

Jared couldn't help his snort of laughter or admiring that Luka was a fierce negotiator. "Go on then."

Luka took off his gloves and fiddled with a lock, and

then opened it to pages filled with scribbles and doodles. Clearly it was a life journal of some sort and could well hold Luka's hopes and dreams.

"Dear Mr. or Mrs. Bryant & Waites," Luka began to read, and then pointed up at the plaque on the building. "I don't know their real names, so I wrote that."

"Good call," Jared praised him.

Luka beamed. "Dear Mr. or Mrs. Bryant & Waites, my Auntie Lee said that you let people borrow boyfriends, and I want one for my dad. It's his birthday next month and I think it would be a nice present because he's very lonely and works awfully hard, and he's always worried about me and I don't know why because I am the best son. I would be kind to a borrowed boyfriend. I wouldn't make a lot of noise, and I would stay over at Auntie Lee's so Dad and his new friend could watch a movie or eat steak." He glanced up at Jared. "Dad loves steak."

"Me too."

"Right, so, eat a steak… okay… thank you very much, love me. I didn't write me, I wrote Luka."

"Of course you did."

"But when I went in there and showed them this they started saying they were calling the police, and one of them was all sappy and patting my head, and I don't want that, I want a boyfriend for Dad, and I want him to smile again."

"How about we take you home and talk about this later."

Luka ignored Jared and instead turned to the back of the journal and pulled out a small plastic bag full of coins and notes. "I have thirty-three dollars and fifty-nine cents to buy a friend for Dad. Is that what you do?"

"What's your address, Luka?"

"Is it enough money?" He was persistent for sure.

"Address first."

Luka shrank into his coat, his enthusiasm visibly leaving him, and he shut the journal. Then gave the street name and number. "I go stay with Auntie Lee when Dad's working. She's our neighbor." He stood and with his journal gripped hard, he took the final steps down. "Thank you anyway," he finished.

Jared was left with a decision to make. An easy one.

He sent a thumbs up to Rowan, then indicated he was going with Luka, and then followed him. Walking Luka wouldn't take him far out of his way, and as soon as he saw Luka safely back then he'd head home. He fell into step with Luka. What should he talk about? He thought about the few things Luka had mentioned. His mom was dead? That's what he'd said, right? And his dad ran a bar? They walked for a while and before Jared got around to breaking the silence, to talk some more, someone shouted Luka's name.

"I'm dead," Luka groaned. "That's my dad."

Chapter Two

"You're in early today?" Nate noted, and slid the filled shot glass across the counter to the man sitting opposite him.

"Closed a big contract this afternoon so thought I'd celebrate." The man grinned, twisted the glass between his finger and thumb. "So, what time do you get off?" He looked at Nate through his blond bangs.

"Eight. Why?" Nate glanced along the bar as the group of women, who'd been there all afternoon, burst into laughter.

"I thought if you were free... maybe we could..."

Ah. Of course. Nate shook his head. "I—"

"Come on. It's been months. We had fun, right? That last time?" he pressed.

Fun, huh? Nate guessed he would call it that, in as much as him and the man at the bar had hooked up a couple of times, all *no strings* sex, when Nate had had an itch in need of scratching, when he was lonely for something being a dad, a bar owner couldn't fill.

Nate dismissed the offer with a smile. "Michael, I'm sorry." He made a point to use the man's name. "But not tonight."

"Why?" Michael downed the shot and pushed the empty glass back toward Nate. "Is it your kid?"

Nate pursed his lips. That wasn't really any of his business. "Another?" he asked, ignoring the question.

"Don't be so cold." Michael chuckled. "He started middle school this year, didn't he? Luka?"

Nate raised an eyebrow.

"Too creepy? I sound creepy, don't I?"

"Maybe a little," Nate said. "More surprised you remember pillow talk from months ago." He wasn't in the habit of talking about Luka to customers.

"What can I say? Memory of an elephant." He smiled. "And that's not all."

Nate laughed. The mood between them lightening. "In your dreams." He straightened and exhaled. "Thank you, but I'm sorry. As you said, Luka's in middle school now. With that and this place, I've a lot going on." Sex had fallen so far down his list of priorities it had almost dropped off completely.

"Then, another time?"

He shrugged. "Maybe." Luka was his priority.

Two things were a must where Luka was concerned. Either Nate's shift at the bar started once he had welcomed Luka home from school or ended, and he was home in time to see his son to bed.

"Excuse me," he said when his cell phone vibrated in his pocket. "Abi, can you watch the bar?" He waved to catch her attention and when she nodded, he slipped into the back room.

"Lee, everything okay?" He glanced at his wristwatch; it was almost five.

"Hi. Yeah. I think." Lee's tone was hesitant. "Is Luka with you?"

As soon as the question was asked it was as if the air had been knocked from him. A knot tightened in his stomach. "You know he isn't." They had settled into a routine; she knew his schedule at the bar.

Lee fell silent.

"Lee? You're kind of scaring me right now."

"Damn it. I knew I should have asked you."

"What are you saying?"

"Luka told me he was going to a friend's house after school."

"Okay." This wasn't the first time Luka had gone to play with friends. "Who? What friend?"

"Erm, Keegan."

Nate pushed the office door shut. "Keegan. Yeah, I know Keegan. He should be on the list of contacts I gave you of his friends."

"Yeah I have his parents' phone number here. But I didn't think anything of it at the time. I mean this kid Keegan was standing right there, face of an angel as he told me Luka was going to go play at his house until dinner time." Lee cleared her throat. "But then, I phoned to ask what time they were bringing him home so I could fix him a meal, 'cause Luka hadn't really said and was in a rush and excited to go hang out with his friend and…"

"And?"

"And they said… They said he hadn't been there. Turns out he'd bribed Keegan with some comic book to get him to say he was going home with him."

Nate pressed his palm to his forehead.

Luka was a good kid. Too good sometimes. Why would he lie?

"Did Keegan say anything else? Like where Luka was actually going? Who he might have gone to see?"

"No. Just that there was something important he had to do."

"No, no, no." What should he do? Police? Was that the right thing to do?

"I'm sure he's fine. You just need to stay calm."

"Calm?" Seriously? She was telling him to calm down. "Calm," he repeated.

Luka's my world. The reason I get up in the morning.

If anything… anything had happened to him…

"He said he'd see me later, that they were playing until dinner time. Wherever he was going, he planned on coming home to eat. What do you want me to do? Should I go look for him?"

Nate crossed the room to pick up his jacket and wallet. "No, you should wait there in case he comes back."

"And you?"

"I'll get a cab, head to the school and I guess home from there. If he's still not turned up after that, then I'll call the police." He paused at the office door. His hand trembled as he reached for the handle.

"Nate?" He'd fallen silent.

He cleared his throat. "I'm fine. I'll call you when I know anything."

"Same," Lee said. "He'll be fine."

"Yeah. Of course he will." He hung up, immediately regretting how abrupt it had been. This wasn't Lee's fault. There was no reason for her not to have believed Luka. It wasn't anything out of the ordinary him playing at a friend's house after school.

What was so different this time?

He filled his lungs and pulled the door open. He raised his hand when Michael was about to say something. He wasn't in the mood for anymore flirtatious banter with a customer. "Abi," he said. "I'm really sorry to have to do this, but I need to go."

"Problem?" she asked.

"I hope not. Will you be okay for a while? I'll call Gregg, see if he can come in earlier, or maybe—"

"I'll be fine." She gave him a firm look. "So, whatever it is just go. Go on." She shooed him.

"Are you sure?" He switched his weight to his other foot.

Abi didn't say anything, just pointed to the door.

"Thanks." He walked around the bar, Michael stopping him, catching hold of his wrist.

"Are you okay?"

Nate nodded. "I have to go. Enjoy your night." He twisted his arm free and jogged for the exit.

The cool early evening air hit him in the face as he stepped outside. He hadn't realized how suffocating the bar had become during Lee's phone call. The walls had closed in and smothered him. He breathed in deeply, pulled on his jacket, and headed for the main street for a cab.

Damn it, Luka, where are you?

Nate wasn't sure he'd ever experienced a sensation such as he did when he spotted Luka on the sidewalk, his anger swept to relief, to a blinding fear over the fact his son was with a fully-grown man. An adult he didn't recognize. He felt sick, a bitter taste rising in his throat. Nate leaned forward. "Can you stop here, please?" He kept his eyes on Luka as they passed him.

The driver grunted, acknowledged Nate's request and pulled up a short way ahead of Luka and whomever he was walking with.

"Thanks." Nate glanced at the fare, grabbed enough bills from his wallet to cover the ride. "Keep the change." He handed over the money and was out of the cab quickly. He needed to get to his son.

"Luka," he yelled and slammed the door shut. He rushed toward Luka, who froze in surprise.

"Dad."

All Nate had wanted to do was wrap Luka in a hug, tell him how worried he'd been, and how much he loved his idiot of a son. But he was blinkered by a feeling of horror. Who was this person standing next to his child?

"Luka." He grabbed Luka by the arm, pulled him away and put himself between his son and the stranger. "What the hell are you doing with my boy?"

The slim man in jeans and a hoodie took a step back. "Easy. This… We were just—"

"Just, what?" He tightened his grip on the thick sleeve of Luka's jacket. He never wanted to let go.

"Dad." He could hear Luka's voice, yet all he could do was focus on the man who had been with him.

"Well?" Nate narrowed his eyes. The man seemed to be younger than him, still in his twenties, and was confused.

"Erm."

"Dad." Luka was tugging on his back. "This is Jared."

"Jared?" Who the hell was Jared? He turned to the man. "Jared. So you spend your day picking up kids? I'm calling the cops!" He pulled out his cell as Jared backed away.

"What? No. Luka was sitting on the steps outside my office, and we were worried, so I was walking him home, I swear that's all."

"Jared's not a bad man," Luka said. He leaned out from behind Nate. "You're not a bad man are you?" he asked more seriously.

"No!" Jared said, then held his hands out in front of him, and then as calm as he could, he added, "No, I'm not. I swear."

Nate swallowed, the tightness in his chest easing a little. "Okay. Jared? I don't even know what's happening anymore."

Jared shook his head as if saying, *don't ask me*. "So, you're Luka's dad?"

"Yes. Nate."

"Hi. I'm Jared. But you know that. Your son was," he pursed his lips, "near my work. Alone. I only wanted to see he got home safely. Nothing else. No bad intentions. I promise." There was a brightness in his eyes that left Nate wanting to believe him.

"Thank you, I guess. Sorry I overreacted."

Jared lowered his hands.

"But you…" Nate turned around and looked down at Luka. "Do you have any idea how worried I was? And Auntie Lee? What were you thinking? Lying? No lies, we don't lie, ever."

Luka's bottom lip trembled. "I'm sorry. I didn't mean to."

Nate held Luka's face, tugged the beanie he was wearing down over his ears. His cheeks flushed pink from the cool air and felt chilled against Nate's warm palms. "What would I do if something happened to you? Hey?" He pulled Luka to him, appreciated the solid feel of him in his arms. "Promise me you won't do anything like this ever again."

There was a small *hic* as Luka nodded against him.

"What were you doing that was so important that you thought you had to lie about it?" He rested his hand on the top of Luka's head, encouraging Luka to lean back.

Luka's eyes were wet, his nose red. "It's your birthday soon. I wanted to get you something."

"What? You didn't have to lie so you could do that."

"It wouldn't be a surprise if I told you."

"Sure, but you didn't have to tell *me*, did you? There's Lee, and your grandpa. Pops would have taken you to buy something if you'd asked him."

Luka pouted. "I wanted to get it myself. Only from me. I saved up."

Nate let out a sigh and the stormy sea of his emotions was finally at peace. "You're an idiot." He smiled and pressed a kiss to Luka's forehead. "I don't care what you give me for my birthday. As long as you're there to spend it with me I'll be the happiest dad in the world." He tapped his finger to Luka's nose. "Got it?"

Luka nodded. "Okay."

"So, we all good now?" Jared said from behind them.

Nate glanced over his shoulder. Jared had his hands crammed into his jacket pockets, and he shifted awkwardly from foot to foot. "I'm sorry. We both are. Aren't we?" He nudged Luka's shoulder.

Luka chewed on his lip then said, "Sorry I bothered you. Thank you for walking me home."

"No worries," Jared said. "But you know, you shouldn't go worrying your dad like that, okay?" Jared hunched his shoulders up toward his ears. "I'm sorry things got weird." He looked at Nate and smiled. "I understand it must have been scary seeing a stranger with your kid."

"'Scary' is one word for it." He bit his lip. "Is there anything I can do to thank you for looking after him?"

"For me?" Jared shook his head. "Knowing he's back where he belongs is plenty." He turned his attention to Luka. "Anyway, pleasure meeting you, Luka. No more sneaking off places without telling somebody first."

"So, I can go if I tell someone?"

Jared opened his mouth. "That's not…" He held his hand over his stomach. "You know what, I'll let your dad handle this one." He stepped back. "I'm going to go. Leave you two to figure things out."

"Wait, let me give you some money or something."

"No, I don't need that."

"Dad?" Nate crouched next to Luka after his insistent tug. "What about dinner?"

"What about it?"

"We could get him dinner."

Nate glanced up at Jared, who was slowly backing away as if he wanted to escape the madness, and who could blame him. He couldn't know that the thought of losing the only bright light in Nate's life had caused him to lose his shit.

"Look, no pressure, but there's a diner right there. Let me buy you a burger at least." Not that he should be treating Luka to his favorite junk food after what had happened. He'd give burgers to his son every day if Luka promised never to disappear again. His heart was still racing, and he swore it was adrenaline that was making him shaky.

"Yay burgers!" Luka said, pulling him back to the present, refocusing on Jared who was scratching the back of his neck and looking adorably confused.

Wait, where did that come from?

"I have to study," Jared began.

Maybe Jared was younger than he seemed if he was studying. "Everyone needs to eat."

"I'm so hungry," Luka pointed out and rubbed his belly to underline the fact.

Nate took hold of Luka's hand and stood. "So, will you join us?"

Jared's gaze drifted downward to where Nate held onto Luka. "Are you sure?"

Luka stared up at Jared. "Please, Jared?" He sounded as if he was going to cry, and his dark eyes were bright. Nate gave his hand a squeeze.

Jared's eyes widened at Luka's plea and then he glanced at the sidewalk, thinking it over. "Okay. Fine."

"Really?" Luka sounded excited.

"Yeah." Jared stepped toward them. "Burgers sounds great."

"I need to text everyone that Luka is okay." He sent out a quick group text, receiving immediate replies of thank god, and a crying face emoji from Lee, followed by an instruction to kiss Luka silly. He settled for patting Luka on the head. "You worried your Auntie Lee, and you owe her an apology."

"Yes, Dad."

"Okay. Burgers." They could eat, say thank you, and then head home.

After all, accounts didn't do themselves.

Chapter Three

Jared had no idea what'd made him say yes, although it probably had a lot to do with the way Luka looked up at him, dark eyes bright with emotion. He was a sucker for kids, and just as susceptible when it came to tears, as proven by many situations where he'd ended up messing up.

It wasn't his fault that he had a soft heart, but he knew it would be the ruin of him one day, and he tried not to want to help everyone in need, but it was hard.

They crossed the street to the upmarket diner, all wooden tables and paper napkins, a perfect place for a real burger, and secretly one of Jared's favorite places to eat after he'd completed a successful job for Bryant & Waites. Well, any booking for them, as they'd not all ended well.

"This table okay?" Luka's dad—*Nate*—asked and gestured to the window with a view, out of the hustle and bustle of tourist traffic. They were lucky, given a review that'd appeared in a *Best Burgers in Manhattan* blog post on the Food Network website. It was a popular place, and every time Jared had been there, it had been heaving with guests. Maybe they'd missed the early dinner rush and were early for the late dinner rush, but the table was free, and they grabbed it.

Nate sat next to the window, Luka next to him, and Jared opposite. This way, Jared could pretend to study the menu while observing the two of them, their interactions incredibly sweet. From a psychological perspective, there was an imbalance to a typical family dynamic. Yes, Nate was the dad, but Luka seemed protective of him, fussing over a missing napkin and leaning super close so he could get a hug. Luka was definitely in trouble, contrite, but Nate had slewed from fear to love and panic to anger in quick flashes of bright color, and was now onto gratitude that Luka was okay, tinged with frustration that it'd happened in the first place. Luka loved his dad, that much was sure, and he respected him. That wasn't just a clinical observation. Luka listened as his dad explained to him for the fourth time why it was a heartbreaking and worrying thing Luka had done, all while hugging him and telling him that he loved him.

Not to mention that Luka had tried his hardest to buy a friend for his dad.

Did Nate need a friend? He seemed to have received a lot of texts from people happy that Luka was okay, and he was easy on the eyes with his thoughtful dark gaze, plump kissable lips, and his soft brown hair. *I bet he has loads of* friends.

"What is it you do, Jared?" Nate asked. "I heard you say studying?"

Jared couldn't help but noticed the wide-eyed stare that Luka was giving him.

"I'm doing my master's in psychology and just finished up a short family services work placement. That's where I'm heading hopefully, working with families, one day."

"How much longer do you have left?"

"I started late, didn't get to college until I was twenty-three, so I don't know, maybe when I'm thirty, which is two years away still." Jared laughed at his words, although the worry that poked inside wasn't something he could ignore.

The waitress arrived to take orders. The Tennessee Burger was a popular choice, with all three of them ordering the smoky barbecue goodness, albeit kid-size for Luka.

"You didn't need to do this," Jared said when the waitress left after filling their water glasses.

"And you didn't need to help my son, but you did. Where did you come across him?"

"He was—"

"You can't tell him," Luka interrupted. "It will spoil his birthday surprise." He added the last part before Nate could stop him, and Jared hid a smile. He wasn't going to spill the details. After all, none of it mattered now, given Luka was safely back with his dad, and they could chalk up the entire incident to a funny thing that'd happened.

"Okay then, it's our secret," Jared said with a smile,

and Luka relaxed. "Luka said you work. Is it round here?"

"Yes, it isn't far. Rhea's Bar, do you know it?"

"The one on East Sixteenth?"

"Yeah, so that's my place." He stopped and glanced at Luka, who was watching him with interest. "Hey, Luka, you want my phone?" He appeared to consider the option of watching Jared and his dad talk or the lure of games on the phone. After a pause, he nodded and then lost himself in *Lemmings*, although Jared noticed he was glancing up every so often to check on the conversation.

"It was what?"

"Mine and my wife's place, but she passed when Luka was younger."

"He told me, I'm sorry for your loss." Jared watched as emotions raced across Nate's face and made his eyes darken momentarily. There was a stiffness in the way Nate controlled his reaction, as if letting himself relax would lead to something awful. "So, yeah, anytime you're over that way, come in, and I'll pour you a beer or make you a fancy cocktail."

"You had me at 'cocktail.'"

"It always works," Nate agreed.

"But you already bought me dinner. You don't have to keep thanking me."

Nate shuddered. "When I imagine what could have happened..." He paused a moment, and a mask of *normal* slipped over his tired expression. "So tell me about you. You're studying psychology, does that mean you're assessing people every time you talk to them?" He smiled widely, putting a protective arm over Luka's shoulder. "Are you doing that to me now?"

This conversation had gone straight past polite hello and where-you-from to banter in a microsecond, and Jared's chest tightened. Many factors influenced attraction, and Jared was already scrutinizing how he and Nate were interacting. There were a ton of tells when attraction existed between two people. Banter and leaning in were two obvious ones, and Jared couldn't even begin to think about the way Nate licked his lower lip. There was a ton of silent messages from Nate. They ranged from an unconscious need to hug his son to the way he wanted to turn the conversation from serious to fun, or that he wouldn't quite meet Jared's gaze. He was nervous, anxious still, and Jared bet his stomach was a ball of nerves. So Jared did what he knew best. He began to manage the situation and forged ahead to find common ground.

He hadn't even realized he was doing it until he opened his mouth and began to talk.

"Do you like to people-watch?" Jared asked. That was always where he began his explanation of psychology to anyone who asked him.

"I work behind a bar. I people-watch all night."

"Okay, so as a barman, you can tell when someone has come in to drown their sorrows, or to celebrate, or to find company. Right?"

"Mostly. You get a feel for it, yes."

"See, that is a skill that you have learned from

countless encounters, and when you're *listening* to people, you're reading them. I do the same kind of thing when I accidentally try and help people without realizing it. Also, it might seem weird when I stare at another person and they see me doing it. So in answer to your question, I can't help assessing on a hundred different things."

For a moment, Jared thought he'd messed up, but then Nate grinned and sat back in his chair. "So what do you see?"

"A dad who loves his son."

Nate pulled Luka close, only letting go when Luka squeaked about the game and how his umbrella wasn't working.

"Daaad," he whined.

Nate pressed a kiss to Luka's hair and then turned to Jared. "That one was easy. Tell me something more."

This was a minefield. There were a ton of non-verbal clues that Jared had picked up, but he wasn't going to mention them.

"I knew your bar was called Rhea's Bar before you told me."

Nate's jaw dropped. "Luka told you?"

"Nope."

"You've seen me there?"

"Nope."

"Then, how?"

Jared pointed at Nate's jersey, a deep amber in color, with a Rhea's Bar logo on his chest, and couldn't help laughing when Nate glanced at the emblem then back up at him with narrowed eyes. "That's cheating."

"Nah, it's just observation."

"What else do you see then?"

Luka had wriggled out of his dad's hold, so Nate was free to lean forward on his elbows, and Jared was lost in his velvet-brown eyes. He wondered if he noticed the brilliance of them because Luka wanted to hire him as a boyfriend for his dad. Were his observations tainted by this flush of attraction he was feeling?

"Okay, so you're a dad, and you work at Rhea's Bar." He counted the two things off on his fingers, "And you don't like baseball."

"How did you… what did I… I didn't say anything about baseball. Luka must have said that because there's no jersey evidence this time."

"Nope, he said nothing. It's all observation. When you came in, you glanced at the television over the bar which is showing an old Yankees game, and you then chose a table and sat with your back to it."

"Maybe I love baseball, and I knew I'd stare at the screen, so I sat facing this way to be polite." Nate rested his chin on his hands, and Jared could see the interest in his gaze—he could've spent all day pretending to be Sherlock Holmes if Nate kept looking at him like that.

"No sports fan, no *real* one anyway, would miss out on the chance of having their beloved sport at least in their peripheral vision. Failing that, to at least comment on what they see, like, oh yeah, this was a close game or something."

"I'll have you know that I'm a very polite person. I never want to appear rude to anyone."

"But I'm right."

Nate bit his lip, holding back a smile, and then shook

his head. "I don't *hate* baseball. It's just that I'm more of a hockey fan. Go Rangers."

"We've been to see them," Luka chimed in. "It was cold and noisy, and I loved it. We had so much popcorn I was almost sick."

"You did not," Nate defended his parenting skills, then grimaced. "It was the hotdog that pushed it over. Anyway, besides you now knowing I let my son eat way too much junk food in hockey stadiums, if that game was on the television, I'd say something. December 8th, 2019, Vegas at the Garden, we won five-nothing, now *that* was a game."

Jared couldn't help smiling at Nate's infectious grin with an added fist pump. He'd fake-dated sports fans before. In the whole Christmas swan incident, the brother of the girl he was fake-dating had been a huge football fan and wore a jersey to the black-tie event. At least he'd had an excuse for his part in releasing the swan because he'd been three sheets to the wind on free champagne after his team had won something or other.

The burgers arrived, and Luka didn't argue when Nate asked for the game of *Lemmings* to end. Whether that was because Luka was hungry or because he just respected his dad, Jared couldn't tell, but dad and son exchanged grins and fell on their respective burgers like hyenas on a fresh kill. They ate the same way, with dedicated silence, until they were halfway through, and then they started to talk. About the weather, homework, Rhea's Bar, it was a mish-mash of everything, and they asked Jared questions. Nate was genuinely interested in Jared's studies and his career aspirations. Plus, he was so damn thankful that he'd been around to rescue Luka, which he repeated often. Luka had chocolate ice-cream for his dessert, pronouncing it the best thing he'd ever tasted and his absolute favorite, and all too soon it was time to leave.

Jared walked with them for a short while, just because he didn't want the dinner part of this meet-up to end. It would be easy to be friends with Nate. Hell, he wasn't going to deny that he felt attraction, but whether he'd ever act on that, given his upcoming exams, was open to debate. Luka tugged him to one side when Nate had to take a call. After securing his journal under one arm, Luka rooted through his pocket and pulled out a handful of coins. They were out of sight of Nate, Luka had made sure of that, and he spoke in a low but urgent voice.

"If I give you two dollars for the dinner thing, will you be my dad's friend another fifteen times?"

"I don't need the money, Luka. I enjoyed the dinner."

His face fell, and tears began to swim in his eyes. "Please," he whispered. "I want him to be happy."

"How about you give it to me next time I see you." Jared had already decided that maybe he'd check out Rhea's Bar, see Nate in his natural environment, maybe talk some more, but he didn't need the payment for friendship.

"No." A single tear spilled on Luka's cheek, and Jared's heart cracked a little. "This is a contract as it said on Mr. and Mrs. Bryant & Waites website."

"Oh, Luka, sweetheart," Jared whispered, and then

in a moment of sheer idiocy, he took the coins and got a hug in return.

And as he waved the little family off, he only had one thought in his head.

What the hell have I agreed to?

Chapter Four

"Luka," Nate called, turning down the volume on the TV.

"Mmm."

"What have I told you? No sleeping in the tub." Nate switched off the television and got to his feet. He sighed as he entered the hallway to find Luka's discarded clothes on the floor outside the bathroom.

"But it's soooo warm and bubbly," Luka mumbled, making a squeaking sound as he slid lower in the bathtub. "And I wasn't sleeping. I'm not tired. I'm relaxing."

Not tired? Nate had been ready to offer Luka matchsticks to prop his eyes open while he was trying to finish his neglected homework before his bath.

"Relaxing, sure." Nate picked up Luka's sweater. He folded it over his arm, smoothing the woolen material. "You know, you sounded like your mom just then. She'd have spent hours in the tub if she could have gotten away with it," he said, smiling fondly at the memory.

"Maybe she was a mermaid," Luka chimed.

"A mermaid, huh?" He separated which of Luka's clothes needed to go into the hamper and which needed to be put away. "She did love the ocean." Memories of the three of them visiting his parents in Florida came to mind. He'd always thought there'd be more vacations, more memories, more time.

There was the sound of splashing, and Nate stuck his head round the door to see Luka had turned onto his stomach, gripping the back of the tub as he kicked his feet in the foamy water.

"What on earth are you doing?"

"Well, if Mom was a mermaid, then I'm half a mermaid."

"Aren't you too big to play mermaid?" Nate shook his head. "Anyway, mermaid or not, it's nearly time for bed. So, hurry up. And don't make a mess."

"Okay." Luka stopped kicking and slipped about in the bath to turn around. He cupped some water in his hands, watching it pour through his separated fingers.

"Ten minutes max," Nate said and caught the cheeky grin that spread across Luka's face. "I'm such a pushover," Nate muttered as he walked to Luka's bedroom.

Having put away Luka's things he made his way to the kitchen and checked his cell phone. Both Abi and Gregg had messaged to assure him everything was going smoothly at Rhea's. They were both hardworking, reliable assets to the bar, and extremely understanding when it came to Luka. Gregg had worked with Nate for a long time, had been the one to call Nate out when he'd buried himself in the work, ignored his grief.

I should find a way to thank them properly.

He placed his cell on the dining table. The bar wasn't his concern for the rest of the evening. His shift would have been over by now, and he'd have been on his way home to see Luka to bed.

He rubbed his brow, heard Luka in the hallway.

"Do you want a hot chocolate?" he called.

"Yes," Luka shouted back, his footsteps loud and fast as he ran toward his bedroom, shutting his door with a bang.

Should he have said more to Luka? Been sterner? Maybe taken away TV privileges or confiscated one of his toys or… He glanced at the board on the wall beside the refrigerator, magnets holding photographs in place.

Rhea, am I really doing things right? He stared at the image of his wife. "You were so much better at this than me."

"Dad?"

Nate cleared his throat and looked over his shoulder. Luka was in his pajamas, his journal hugged to his chest, and a towel over his head. "Sit down." He waited for Luka to get on his chair, then stood behind him. He rubbed the towel over Luka's hair.

"Ahhhhhh, th-th-thanks, Da-ad."

Nate laughed. "You're welcome." He gave Luka a brief squeeze. He hung the towel on the back of the chair. "Let's get you that hot chocolate."

Luka sat in silence, only speaking when Nate placed

the full mug on the table in front of him. "Marshmallows?" Luka asked in a small voice.

"Do you think you deserve marshmallows?"

With a thoughtful expression, Luka tilted his head, as if thinking about his answer. "I don't know. Maybe." He gave a small smile, which faded when he met Nate's eyes. He shook his head. "No.

"No." Nate sighed and pulled out the chair on the opposite side of the table. "But next time. You can have marshmallows next time." He sat down.

Luka hugged the mug of cocoa and blew across the hot liquid's surface. "'Next time,'" he repeated happily.

Nate rubbed at the pain in his chest as he sat with Luka. "You really scared me today." He didn't want to upset Luka again, but sitting there, watching his son, the sense of loss that could have been swelled inside him. "I love you. Pops and Nana Kay, Lee, too. They'd all be sad if something bad had happened to you."

Luka ducked his head, as if trying to hide behind his mug.

"I can still see you." Nate leaned forward and touched the back of Luka's hand. He needed Luka to understand how important he was. Nothing mattered more than him. "I don't need surprises and presents from you. Those can wait until you're older. For now, you, happy and healthy is everything I need for my birthdays, okay?"

"That's silly."

"It's the truth." He gripped Luka's hand then released it. "Though, if you want to get me a big bag of M&Ms, I wouldn't say no, but *only* if you go with Lee to

get them. No more lying and no more wandering off
places by yourself. You were lucky Jared was such a nice
guy."

Luka lifted his head. "Do you like him?"

"Who? Jared?"

"I liked him. He was cool." Luka picked up his mug,
blew some more before flicking his tongue out and
testing the heat of his drink.

"Sure, I liked him." As much as anyone he'd met for
the first time. Jared's adorable confusion had certainly
endeared him to Nate. Spending time in his company
had been easier than Nate had expected, maybe because
he was unfamiliar, didn't know all the baggage of Nate's
past. Jared had been someone new, and brought with
him new conversation, new experiences, new feelings. "I
guess he was kinda cool."

Luka smiled, then lowered his drink, reaching for his
journal. Loose sheets of paper were stuffed between the
pages.

Has he filled it again?

"Do you need a new one?" Nate couldn't remember
how long Luka had been carrying around the same
journal. He loved to write and draw and sometimes
jotted down his feelings among it all. Nate didn't pry, it
didn't feel right to, but occasionally, Luka would come to
him, show him what he'd been up to.

*I'm curious, but that's his own little world to populate with his
thoughts and feelings.*

He hoped there would never be a day he worried so
much about his son he would need to invade those
private scribblings.

"No. It's not full, but I did something." Luka opened the journal. "I wrote this for Jared." He slid out one of the pieces of paper and held it out.

"What is it?"

"A letter."

"For Jared? That's sweet, but—"

"And one for Lee and Gregg and you, too." He held out more sheets.

Nate took the notes. He glanced at Lee's then Gregg's, both contained an apology, to Lee for lying and to Gregg for making him come into work early. He tucked them to the back of the pile and stared at the one for Jared. He scanned the lines of thanks Luka had written. Thanks for walking him home, thanks for being nice, thanks for coming to dinner, thanks for talking to his dad.

"When did you write these?"

"Before I got in the bathtub."

"I thought you were doing homework?"

Luka gave a teeth flashing smile. "I did that, too."

"Really?"

Luka nodded. "I only had math."

"Okay," Nate said. He wasn't wholly convinced but after today he wanted to trust Luka wouldn't lie to him again.

"I'll drop Lee's to her once you've gone to bed, and I'll give Gregg his when I see him next."

"And Jared's."

Nate pursed his lips. "I don't know if that's possible."

"But you told him to come to the bar," Luka stated.

"I did?"

"For a cocktail."

"I thought you were busy playing games on my phone." Nate scratched the back of his neck, tried to remember exactly what they'd talked about. The beginning of dinner was a bit of a blur, his heart still racing, his mind unsettled. "I guess I did." It had been a general invitation out of politeness, there was no reason Jared would take him up on the offer. There was no guarantee he'd see Jared again.

"So, make sure you give it to him."

"Luka."

Luka stared at him with a determined expression.

"All right." Nate nodded. "Sure. If he stops by the bar, I'll pass on your letter." He turned to the note intended for him, smiled at the strange little sketch at the bottom of the page. "What's this supposed to be?"

"What do you mean? That's a burger."

"Ah, so it is. So, this is..." He eyed the three figures in a row.

"Me and you and Jared getting burgers."

Nate laughed. "But there's only one burger. I don't remember sharing one burger."

"Dad." Luka frowned. "Stop being mean."

"Sorry. It's lovely." He glanced at the apology that preceded the drawing, the word *sorry* taking up a good chunk of the page in bold capital letters. "Thank you."

They sat together, talking about nonsense, about what Luka had been doing at school, until he had finished his drink.

"Done," Luka said and wiped his mouth with the back of his hand.

"Go brush your teeth and get into bed. I'll come through in a minute."

Luka grabbed his journal and yawned. "Okay."

Nate rinsed out Luka's mug and put it on the side. He'd deal with it thoroughly with the breakfast dishes. He stopped by the sink and stared at his reflection in the window. He closed his eyes. His head felt heavy. Why was he exhausted? It was as if he was crashing after pulling an all-nighter at the bar. He rubbed his eyes. He'd intended to look over the business accounts once Luka was in bed, but the way he was feeling, he might just grab a shower and head to his own.

"Dad."

"Coming." Nate wiped his face, then made his way to Luka's room. The plaque on his door was still the original one Rhea had bought when Luka was born, a baby giraffe in a diaper sitting alongside Luka's name, backed by trees and the sun, and a pair of birds sitting atop the *L*. "Did you prepare your books and things for school tomorrow?"

"Yep," Luka said and jumped onto the bed.

"Have you set your alarm?"

"Yup," Luka grinned.

Nate watched in amusement as Luka turned in a circle on his knees, threw one of his pillows to the floor as well as the collection of stuffed animals, then scooted beneath the comforter. "Are you in?"

After some wriggling, Luka pulled the bedding up to his chin and lay still. "I'm in."

"You sure? Want to squirm about a bit more?"

"No. I'm done."

Nate leaned over and pressed a kiss to Luka's forehead. "Love you."

"Dad?" Luka said when Nate stood. "Love you, too."

Nate smiled. "I know." He walked to the door, flicking the light switch as he passed. "See you in the morning."

"Night," Luka said, rolling over to face the wall.

Nate pulled the door to, leaving a crack of light to shine into the room. He gazed at his son for a moment, then went back to the kitchen. It was getting late to be knocking on Lee's door, so instead he laid the letter Luka had written on the table and picked up his phone. He twisted the note until his shadow wasn't covering it and snapped a picture. He opened the messaging app and sent the image to Lee, who replied quickly with a smiling emoji and another apology of her own.

It's fine. Not your fault. I've told him no going to play with friends for a while. He shouldn't ask, but if he does tell him no. Thanks for everything, he replied.

The letters for Gregg and Jared he folded and tucked inside his jacket pocket. There was no way he could promise Luka he'd deliver the one to Jared, but he figured the chance of seeing him wasn't zero. Maybe he would visit the bar at some point. He glanced down at his hand as guilt prickled his skin, and he found he was already twisting the silver band on his ring finger, a habit he'd acquired, a way to ground himself in the quiet moments when it was only him and his thoughts.

He ran his hand through his hair and considered what had happened with Luka. Maybe he should cut back on a shift or two for a while. Spend some extra time with him. He picked up his cellphone and scrolled through his contacts before making a call.

"Hey, Don," Nate said and pushed closed the kitchen door so not to disturb Luka.

"Oh, Nate, it's you. And what do you mean Don?"

Nate sat at the table. "Sorry, Pops." He leaned back in his seat. His father-in-law was known by Pops by just about everyone, his nickname since way back when he ran a bar with one of his friends who was an ex-cop.

"So, what's up? Is it money? You need money? Luka need something?"

"Not money."

"You sure? I've told you before, you need only ask."

"Thanks, but that's not it." He chewed on his thumbnail. "You know how you and Kay dropped not so subtle hints about you getting under her feet and you missing your bar since you retired?"

Pops cleared his throat. "Oh, you caught that. Look, I don't want to tread on toes. That bar is yours and Rhea's. Was. Still is. It was just an old man reminiscing the good old days."

"No. That's not... You wouldn't be... treading on toes. Um, it wouldn't be much. A couple of hours here and there."

"Are you being serious?"

"Yeah. But if I got it wrong..."

"No. No. I'd love to."

"Great. I'll check things out and get in touch soon."

"I appreciate it." Pops paused, then asked, "But you're okay? You and Luka?"

Nate looked at the ceiling. "We are. Sorry if I sound tired or anything. Long day."

"You do, a little. Anyway, I'll let you rest and talk soon."

Nate sat forward. "Sure. Goodnight. Bye." He hung up, rested his head in his hand as he eyed the family photographs beside the refrigerator.

Rhea, I'm so tired.

Chapter Five

As soon as Jared stepped inside Rhea's Bar he went into default setting and began to catalogue the clientele. There were a few tables along the wall, cozy spaces with soft lighting and a brighter space near the bar with stools, and light reflecting from hundreds of bottles on glass shelves. He couldn't see Nate but took a stool and waited his turn to talk to the gray-haired barman serving a woman who was chatting about the weather, and the promise of late snow, and how her boyfriend loved the snow, apparently more than he loved her.

"It's his loss, Emily," the barman said seriously, "find someone who loves you more than snow." He gave an exaggerated sigh. "If only I wasn't married and twenty years younger." By the time she left to take a seat with a friend, balancing two cocktails, she was smiling. The barman was good, Jared could see that.

"Evening," he said. "What can I get you?"

Jared followed the barman's gesture to a board on the wall to a specials list handwritten with precision on a chalk board. Tonight's alcohol of choice was vodka, and he was torn between going for a cocktail or just asking for a beer. Only this place screamed new adventures, he had money burning a hole in his wallet, and the description of a Madras, orange and cranberry juices with vodka, seemed a good place to start. He refused to be disappointed that Nate wasn't behind the bar, but maybe it was for the best, because getting involved with Nate and by extension Luka was never going to end in any other way than complicated.

Even though he'd agreed with Luka that he'd be his father's friend, there were sparks of attraction between him and Nate that he couldn't ignore, and he had to admit that the last thing he needed right now was complications. Work on two essays due in by the end of the month fought for time with more reading, and lectures. Not to mention the next boyfriend hire was in prep stage, which meant Rowan emailing Jared a shit ton of reading material. Each booking had to be perfect because that was what clients paid Bryant & Waites for, and Jared was happy to do the research, it was just a matter of fitting it in with everything else.

So yeah, being there was the last thing he should've been doing, but the two dollars were in his pocket and he'd never been more aware of a contract.

"I'll take a Madras." He finally decided, and the older man sporting an apron in the same colors as the jersey that Nate had been wearing collected what he needed. There was a theme to Rhea's, the deep reds, leather, wood. Every conceivable kind of alcohol seemed to be on display with bottles lining glass cabinets behind the bar. Jared turned to check out the room, watching a couple at the far table locked in a kiss, the small group of businesspeople all talking over each other, and the two others sitting on the stools at the bar. It was easy to imagine that this was the kind of warm and welcoming place that made people stay, maybe for two or three more cocktails?

"Here you go."

Jared turned back to the barman, and handed over the money, putting the change in the tip jar as if he had all the money in the world.

"Is Nate not in tonight?"

The man's glance sharpened in that assessing way where Jared knew he was being judged and possibly found wanting all in one go. Then the narrow-eyed glance relaxed as the barman appeared to come to some kind of decision.

"Who's asking?"

Jared held out a hand, which the barman took immediately, his grip firm. "Jared, I'm a friend of Nate's. And Luka as well." He didn't know why he added that last part, but it was true. Luka and Nate were mixed together in his head and he doubted that he could stay away from the little family and not see them as a whole.

The barman's eyes widened, and he let out a soft expletive. "You're kidding me, Jared, right? From the other day?"

He guessed that was the whole Luka thing that was being referred to. "Uh huh." The barman did something Jared hadn't expected. He tugged him to lean over the bar and then manhandled him into a sideways hug.

"I'm Luka's grandfather, call me Pops, and thank you for finding him. You should have said who you were, I wouldn't have charged you for the drink."

"I'm not taking more free stuff," Jared protested, even as Pops released him and let out a bellowing laugh.

"Luka was right," he said and winked.

"Right about what?"

"Nothing, nothing, Nate's out back. Hang on." He pressed something under the counter and a door swung open at the shadowy end of the bar, Nate rushing out.

"What's up, Pops?" He was checking around as if he was expecting some great problem but relaxed just before he saw Jared at the bar, grinning instantly.

"You're here," he said. "Pops, this is Jared, he's the one who found Luka."

"I know. Here," Pops slid a glass of Sprite over to Jared then ushered Nate out from behind the bar. "Sit, talk. You spend too much time in the books and don't have enough fun."

It didn't seem as if Nate was a hundred percent behind the suggestion and was going to disagree, but Pops sent him a look that not only spoke volumes but had Nate admitting defeat and then leading Jared to a table in the corner.

"He says I work too hard," Nate murmured as they sat, "he's probably got a point." He relaxed back in the chair, exhaling, and then cracking his neck and sighing again. "Sometimes I stare and stare, and the numbers just don't add up."

Was Nate talking about literal numbers? Like the hours that made up his life? Both explanations seemed reasonable. "Add in percentages and they literally don't add up. One supplier has placed stock with us, on the understanding we give feedback on sales. I can give them the money figure, but they're all about upsell, and asking how they can help to support me, and I have no freaking idea. I'm behind the bar, and people buy drinks, or they don't, so how in god's name do I put a figure on estimated sales and what might affect them." He shook his head. "Rhea always used to…" He scrubbed his face, and then made a visible effort to pull himself out of his cycle of worry and into the present. "Sorry, ignore me."

"Percentages are my jam."

Nate looked at him disbelieving. "You're smiling. *No one* thinks that about percentages and smiles."

"There's a whole component in my studies on statistics, and that includes percentages, so I guess I learned to love them."

"Why would they be part of studying psychology?"

"Expectation against managing reality."

Nate bit his lip as if he was keeping back a smile. "That's deep."

"I'm a deep kind of guy." Jared smirked and brushed his shoulders.

Nate sipped his Sprite, then placed the glass back on the coaster. "I just have all these numbers in my head, and if only I could make sense of them."

"I could help you if you want?" Jared joked, his

voice low and growly. Nate's eyes widened and after the longest long pause he cleared his throat.

"Maybe, but I don't know how you'll help, god knows why someone who walks in here picks a particular drink."

"Okay, I like a good challenge." Jared shuffled his chair to sit diagonally, but next to Nate, so they had a view of the bar. He couldn't let himself think about the fact he was close enough to Nate to reach out and touch him. *Kiss him.*

"What do you mean?"

"Well. Look at it this way. Imagine all those random people who don't know you or the bar, we can use percentage possibilities to suggest what order when they come inside. Take all the types of alcohol and the number of people and if they all chose equally then—"

"You lost me at 'random.'"

"Okay, look at it this way. I think there's an eighty percent likelihood that the next person at the bar will order a vodka-based cocktail."

"That's kind of specific for a guess." Nate chuckled.

"Well, I can't be specific, but I think it's got to be high."

"It's not a fair test surely, because we're advertising vodka week on social media and there's a poster on the door so people who come in might already want vodka, and what about the ones who don't want alcohol at all?" He gestured at his Sprite.

"You're right, but when they get here, they're faced with a lot more choices. Only when they order... just watch," Jared gestured at the newest customers, two guys chatting about something that made them smile at each other, still talking as they took off their coats, then leaning on the bar ready to order. "See what Pops does."

They watched as Pops asked what the guys wanted and then gestured to the board with the vodka specials with a broad welcoming smile before placing out some snacks and chatting about something they couldn't hear from where they sat.

"See? He's showing that he's happy to have them here, then he asks them what they want which means they could choose any combination of drinks in the entire bar. He guides them to a choice and makes a subtle gesture to focus them in on how the vodka drinks are on special. We all like to think we know our own minds, but we're influenced by things we don't even see. The kind of numbers your supplier wants is likely all about understanding the human factor. I'm rambling now."

"Okay, I think I get it." Nate was lying.

They exchanged smiles.

At this point Jared should really have shuffled his chair back, but he liked it here, tucked into the corner talking. It helped that their elbows knocked, and that Nate didn't make an effort to move away. He couldn't pull himself from the attraction flaring between them.

Nate filled the silence. "So you met Pops then? He's Rhea's dad and used to own a bar of his own way back. He's been retired from the bar business for years now, helped Rhea and me find this place. Luka is at football practice, then dinner at Lee's, so Pops came over to give me time to get caught up on the accounts." He sounded defensive—was that because of Luka, or because he felt awkward that Rhea's dad was behind the bar? There were so many complicated layers to Nate, and Jared couldn't wait to peel them back.

Nate shook his head. "What happened the other day was a wake-up call—I should have known that Luka was... well there's no point going back over it." He scrubbed his hands over his face again, and Jared wished he could say something that made Nate look less tired. "Anyway, it's good to take a break."

The sharp change in conversation threw Jared for a moment but he sipped his drink then made an exaggerated appraisal of the taste before setting his glass down again.

"That's just what I needed, and I've had my head in books all day, so a break was called for."

They sat in silence for a while, and Jared tried not to stare, but he couldn't avoid seeing the exhaustion lining Nate's face, nor the dark smudges beneath his eyes. Juggling being a dad with running this bar, then add in percentages, and it seemed as if he was on the edge.

"It's been a long time since I've just stopped to talk to a... friend," Nate admitted and picked at the seam of his pants as if his admission had cost him something and he didn't want to see Jared's reaction.

Jared knocked his elbow. "I'm good at being a friend. Ask my roommate Ethan who relies on me to dig him out of all kinds of situations."

"Like what?"

"Don't ask. He's the nicest guy on the planet, a scientist, but he has the worst taste in men. Last month he dated a fellow scientist who was actually experimenting on him."

"For real?"

"It was only a blind study for something or other super clever that I don't understand, but apparently it was a very bad thing. Worst is Ethan is in a world of his own, so I look out for him."

"Then you are a good friend."

"I try to be, so what if I took a look at your report and helped you give the supplier what they need to hear. Would that help?"

Nate frowned. "Is that like you asking to see my etchings? Because I'm not interested in *anything* right now that isn't just talking. I have too much to think about, I'm too tired, and… I'm rambling aren't I?"

Jared couldn't take his eyes off Nate, his gaze moving to the lush mouth, then back up from the smile to Nate's wry expression. Something tugged inside him, a need to hug Nate and tell him it was okay, and that he had enough on his plate to consider anything other than friendship. Between studying and work, he was tired as well—just not as tired as Nate.

"Do you even have etchings?" he asked after a short moment, and it was enough to raise a smile.

"No, but I have percentages."

"I can help." Jared veered away from teasing and flirting to just being one of the good guys. Nate glanced at the office door, and Jared could see the concern in his eyes. Given the size of this place it was probably a very small office. "You want to bring it out here and I can look?"

Nate stared at him, and Jared could see all the questions in his expression and held his breath. What he'd just done was confirm that he too was okay with friends, and that he was here to help. After a pause, Nate nodded. "Yeah."

He went into his office then came back out bearing a notebook, a folder, and a calculator, then set up on the table.

"Welcome to my world," Nate murmured as he sat, then opened the book and shuffled it Jared's way.

Jared held his hand out for the pen, pulled over the calculator, and glanced at the figures.

"Okay then, let's do this." Jared remained upbeat, but Nate frowned and stared at the paper as if it was going to bite him. As Jared explained the calculation, and added wording about expectation versus reality, the frown cleared, and by the end of it Nate was still confused, but it appeared as if some of the weight had been lifted.

"Thank you," he said with a half yawn, and then rested back in the chair. "I mean it."

Jared fought the urge to pat his hand, or casually touch his arm. They'd set boundaries, and now they just had to stick to them.

Easy. Right?

Chapter Six

"Can I get you another drink? As thanks?" Nate closed the folder, rubbing his palms over the red plastic cover.

"There's no need." Jared rested his head in his hand and smiled. "Just happy I could help."

He smiles so easily, so warmly.

"You did," Nate said.

Jared had gotten a little ahead of himself in places, diving too deep into the numbers and stripping the calculations back, trying to explain the why and theory behind them. Nate was more learn-a-method-and-repeat, but with different numbers, when it came to anything math-related.

Jared chuckled. "Good." He ran his fingers up and down his empty glass, the motion capturing Nate's attention.

Jared was a good-looking guy, gorgeous eyes, pouty lips, flirty body language, and a killer smile that would make anyone melt.

What am I even thinking? Nate felt hot suddenly. *I don't have time to melt. Too much to do.* And besides, if it was just about sex, he was able to find a fix for that. He was sure Michael, or somebody else could help him to satisfy those needs.

He stared at Jared. What drew him to Jared wasn't the same as to someone like Michael. Being around Jared was different. It was as if he was being seen, *all* of him, not just physical desire, and against his better judgement he'd taken an interest in Jared in return. Jared was giving him something he'd been missing, and it was comfortable, but at the same time, kind of scary.

How much of me does he actually see? The father, the bar owner, the tired, scared, lonely man?

Nate cleared his throat and pointed to Jared's glass. "Are you sure I can't get you another? If it makes you feel better, I'll even let you pay for it."

Jared met his eyes. "Thanks, but I should head out. I have an assignment or two due, as well as some work stuff." He pushed his glass away and sat back, readying himself to leave his seat.

"Sounds tough," Nate said.

"Not as tough as running this place, I'm sure." He got to his feet, and Nate did the same. "You'll say hi to Luka for me, won't you? He seems like a good kid."

"He is, usually, and of course I will." Nate gathered his things. He felt there was something he was forgetting. "Oh, that's right. I have something for you."

Jared shook his head. "Honestly, I don't want anything."

"*This* you have to take. Just wait here for a moment." He pointed at the table. "Sit. I'll be right back."

"Okay." Jared was confused but obediently sat back down.

"Two minutes." Nate didn't explain further and headed to the office. He sighed as he glanced around the small space. The once ordered shelves had fallen into disarray over the years, their guardian no longer around to keep them in check.

"Where is it," he mumbled to himself. He had brought to work the letters Luka had written. He had already handed over the one to Gregg, who had briefly glanced at it and grinned before crumpling it up and tucking it into the back pocket of his pants. The letter for Jared, Nate had left on his desk, which was covered in disheveled piles of folders and paperwork.

Great. He moved a few things, then checked the desk drawer, relieved to find the folded letter on top of a pile of pens and post-its.

He picked up the piece of paper, checked the letter's contents. Luka would be happy to know he was able to deliver it. He took a deep breath then returned to Jared.

"Here," he said and held out the note.

Jared took it from him. "This is…?"

"You'll see." He slid back in the seat facing Jared.

Jared chuckled. "From Luka. That's sweet." He met Nate's eyes. "Sweet kid. Please thank him for me."

"Sure." Nate worried his lower lip. "I know I've said it plenty of times already, but truly, thank you. For the other day, and just now."

"You're welcome." Jared leaned forward, and for a moment Nate thought he was going to reach over and take his hand.

Nate swallowed back the lump that formed in his throat. Was he disappointed? If so, about what? What did he want from Jared or his touch? A friend? Comfort? Someone who'd rub his arm and tell him everything was going to be okay? That he was doing a good job?

It wasn't as if he hadn't heard those kinds of words before. Don, Kay, Lee, even Gregg and Abi. But in some ways, it felt as if those were said out of obligation. Jared was practically a stranger, a fresh perspective, a psychology student who maybe saw truths others didn't.

Nate clasped his hands together. It wasn't as if Jared had that kind of superpower.

"Anyway." Jared sat back. "I should go, but, if it's okay with you, maybe I could stop by for another cocktail some time?"

It was nice to relax and chat with adult company. Nate didn't do it often enough. He had no siblings, his parents were down in Florida living the high life of their retirement, Don and Kay, though family, weren't *his*, and if not for Luka, since Rhea's passing, would they care as much as they did? Lee was his neighbor, a godsend where Luka was concerned, but a neighbor nonetheless, and before friendship, Gregg and Abi were his employees.

The other adults in his life had been infrequent, brief, physical connections, whose names and faces he doubted he could recall now. He'd never wanted anyone but Rhea. She'd been the only woman he ever loved.

Maybe she will be forever. The only one.

It wasn't as if he hadn't noticed his preference for male sex partners.

"Are you okay?" Jared asked when Nate didn't answer.

"What? Oh, yes. Sorry. I think I still have numbers swirling in my head." He laughed it off. "But yes, definitely. You should come again and bring your friends." He met Jared's eyes. "You know they can help my percentages by buying lots of cocktails."

Jared nodded. "Sounds good." He did reach out this time, touching the top of Nate's arm. "Take care. I'll see you again."

"Okay." Nate folded his arms across his chest, lifting one of his hands to wave when Jared glanced back at him. "Bye," he mouthed. He relaxed his shoulders when the bar door swung closed behind Jared.

"He's gone?" Pops said from behind Nate, as he collected the empty glasses.

"Yeah. He had something to do." Nate turned his head, glanced at the clock on the wall behind the bar. "I should probably get going as well. Are you sure you'll be all right?"

Pops quirked an eyebrow. "Who do you think I am?"

"Retired." Nate grinned.

"I see now. Luka seems to think he's funny, too. Must get it from you."

Nate rubbed the back of his neck. "But, seriously, are you sure this is okay?"

"You said you wanted to spend some extra time with Luka, what's not to be sure about? Besides, I have your very capable staff on hand if I forget how to pour a beer."

Nate lowered his head. "Thanks. But promise me,

you'll tell me if I'm asking too much. Last thing I need is Kay on my case."

Pops drew a cross over his heart with his free hand. "Trust me, I don't want my wife on my case either."

Nate nodded. "Okay."

"So, will Jared be coming again?" Pops asked, resting a hand on his hip, his gaze settling beyond Nate toward the exit.

"I don't know. He said he might."

"Maybe when he gets thirsty, hey?" Pops laughed.

Nate exhaled through his nose. "Maybe."

"He seemed like a great guy. Friendly. Straightforward."

"He is. Well, I think he is." Nate smiled. "Luka seems to like him."

Pops looked at Nate thoughtfully. "I've missed that, you know?" He raised the hand in which he held the empty glasses.

"Missed what?"

"You, smiling. Don't see it enough these days. And certainly not that kind of smile."

That kind? What did that even mean?

"I don't get it." He smiled plenty, didn't he?

"You know. *That* smile. It was the one you used to have whenever you looked at my Rhea."

Guilt ached in Nate's chest. He unfolded his arms, gripped his ring finger. "Don, that's not... " He was surprised when Pops wrapped his hand around his and stopped the twisting of his wedding band.

"It's been four years, Nate. It's okay to show that smile for another person. It would have been okay even before now. I'm not saying it should be Jared, I'm not saying it has to be anyone, not if you don't feel ready. I'm just saying, she wouldn't mind if you found someone you wanted to smile for. I just want you to remember that."

Nate tensed his jaw. The bite of grief tightened in the back of his throat. He gripped his ring, resisted the urge to free his hand from beneath Pops'.

"Sorry," Pops said and withdrew his hand. "You know I've crossed the line when you start calling me Don again."

Nate shook his head. "It's not you it's… I know Rhea wasn't like that. She wasn't petty or spiteful. I know it but still, sometimes…" He released his hand, stretched his fingers. The dim lights of the bar highlighted the scratches from years of wear on the ring's silver surface. "It's hard."

"Go home," Pops said.

"You about to tell me my face will make the beer taste bad?" Nate tried to lift himself out of the thick black tar he felt as if he was sinking into.

"No, but Luka is waiting for you, right? Go see your son."

Nate nodded. "Yeah." A small smile twitched at the corner of his mouth. Luka was his reason for not sinking beneath the surface.

Seeing Luka was *exactly* what he needed.

"Dad, I'm done."

Nate twisted the science workbook. "You want me to check it?"

"I'm fine. Mrs. Bridges says I'm good at science." He put his pencils into his pencil case. "I got full marks in the experiment we did last week, and I got three smiley face stickers in class."

"Are there frowny face stickers, too?"

Luka closed his book, rested his chin on the edge of the table. "I don't know. I'm too awesome."

Nate laughed. "So modest."

"You should ask at the next parent-teacher conference."

"Another one? There's only so many times I can be told what an amazing son I have." He leaned back to rest on his elbows. The two of them sat next to each other on the floor at the coffee table.

"Do you want me to skip class or something?" Luka raised his eyes, dimples in his cheeks as he grinned.

"Don't you dare. As you said. You're awesome so let's keep it that way."

"Okay," he said.

Nate checked the time on his cellphone. "So, what now? You've ninety minutes until bedtime. A movie? Video games? Board games?"

Luka pouted as he considered his choice. "Mouse Trap or Guess Who or Battleships. Or all of them."

"Really?"

Luka looked at him with doe eyes.

"Fine. If you're quick."

"Yes." Luka whooped as he scrambled to his feet and ran toward his bedroom.

Nate chuckled and leaned back to stare at the ceiling. He was calmer than before, what Pops had said, mixed with his own feelings from hanging out with Jared had sent him spiraling. Could he really move on with someone new? He'd fought against it all this time, used Luka and the bar as excuses to keep his heart closed to the possibility of loving someone else.

It's okay just the two of us. Me and Luka, we just need each other.

He lowered his head when he heard Luka come back into the room, a pile of game boxes in his arms.

This way is better, right? Nate's thoughts betrayed him as Jared, his smile, continued to linger in the back of his mind.

"So, which one first?" Nate sat forward. Jared wasn't here, Luka was.

Luka pointed at each box in turn then settled on the middle box. "Mouse Trap."

"Come here a minute," Nate said.

Luka crawled over. "What?"

"Closer."

Luka sighed but came nearer, yelping then laughing when Nate grabbed him and pulled him into a tight hug.

"Ah, this is nice. Luka hugs," Nate said and nuzzled into the crease of Luka's neck. Time with his son was the most important thing to him.

"Itchy." Luka tensed, raising his shoulder to his ear to squeeze Nate out of the space. He giggled as he squirmed, slipping down until he was out of Nate's hold and laid on the floor. He lay there coughing as he caught his breath.

"You all right down there?" Nate ruffled Luka's hair.

Luka nodded and scrambled back to the coffee table. He tipped up the box, emptying its contents onto the table. "You help, too," he insisted and threw the sheet of instructions toward Nate, only for the paper to twist back in his direction and he grumbled.

"Coming," Nate said and shuffled forward. He smiled as Luka spread out the various Mouse Trap parts. "So, which bit first?"

"You look after these," Luka said and pushed the player pieces over to him.

"Yes, boss," Nate teased and Luka grinned.

Yeah. This is fine.

Chapter Seven

The call woke Jared from a vodka-and-kisses kind of dream, and for the longest time he ignored the discordant buzzing, but the damn thing kept going until the noise fractured the warm and fuzzies he had going on and pulled him awake. Bleary-eyed, he searched for the cell, which he was sure had been right next to him but had slipped into the top drawer when he'd shoved the lube back. So much for getting off to the images in his head, then sleeping and losing himself in sexy dreams that had lasted all night long.

Moving the cell made the screen light up and he groaned and fell back on the pillow. Ethan. Three missed calls and five texts, plus ten notifications in their chat. He called him straight back, because Ethan was not only his closest friend but also his roommate, and if there were phone calls and texts and messages then there was also trouble. Ethan was synonymous with trouble, either with chemistry gone wrong or his dating messes.

"What's wrong, Ethan?" Last he'd known, Ethan had been having dinner with his latest love, Marcus something or other, an accountant who Ethan assured Jared was *not* married.

There was some banging and crashing and then a woman's voice on the phone.

"Is this Jared Williams?"

"Speaking." Jared sat up in bed. For all Ethan's mishaps, he'd always answered calls, and this sounded way more official than his idiot best friend.

"This is Officer Lester. We have Ethan Cooper here and he's asking for you."

"Here where?" Jared swung his legs to the floor then stood, already pulling clean underwear out of the drawer and doing the one-legged dance as he listened to the woman talk.

"We'd like you to come collect your friend from St Marks Memorial."

"What's he doing there? Is he hurt?" Fear settled in Jared's chest.

"No," Officer Lester explained. "He's here because I'm purple, and he said you are listed as his next of kin."

Jared pulled the phone away from his ear and stared at it, wondering if maybe he was still asleep. Next of kin sounded way more dramatic than just emergency contact. What did she mean she was purple? She was still talking, but even on speaker phone, as he dressed, she wasn't making much sense. Something about a boyfriend, and did Jared know what Ethan had been planning, and did he know how much a Lexus cost? Jared certainly *didn't* know how much a Lexus cost, given he'd never owned a car. After all, the train tracks ran right from college to his shared place with Ethan, and nobody needed a car in the city.

"… doesn't want to press charges, but if you don't get here soon I might arrest him myself."

Jared called a cab and made it to St Marks in record time because there wasn't much in the way of traffic at three a.m., sliding to a halt in reception and looking for god knows what.

"Mr. Williams?"

He spun to face the woman who'd spoken, a cop in uniform with the name *Lester* on her badge, but it wasn't that which made Jared stop, it was the fact that half her face was purple, and most of her uniform. In fact there was a distinct pattern on her skin where it was clear she'd thrown up a hand to cover herself.

"Me, I'm Mr. Williams, Jared."

"This way." She led him down a corridor and through doors until Jared was all turned around. They arrived at a visitors' room, and she shoved open the door. "He's all yours, take him home. Now."

"Jared! You came!" Ethan sounded like a kid meeting Santa, jumping to his feet, hugging Jared hard, then grabbing the bags on the seat next to him. "Let's go."

Jared decided there and then questions would wait, given Officer Lester had her hand on her belt and her purple-colored expression was dour. He hurried Ethan out of the room and then near-dragged him down the corridors, attempting to recall the way he'd come, and then they were outside the hospital, Ethan looking up at him with his patented puppy dog lost expression.

"Whoops," he said with a forced smile.

"What happened, Ethan?" Jared couldn't wait to hear the latest story. Ethan mad-scientist-in-the-making went from one guy to another, forgot about them when he was deep in experiments, and nearly always ended up getting himself in trouble.

"Thank you for coming to get me."

"Don't change the subject."

Ethan clutched his bags to his chest. "Marcus lied to me. He was married," he said, and Jared touched his arm in reassurance because even though Ethan kept doing this to himself, Jared wasn't going to be a shitty friend and say *I told you so*. "He had all this baggage, kids, three ex-wives, but he swore to me that he was free now, to be with me. But he lied. I was running an experiment, and there was this purple byproduct... I mean, it's harmless, but I took it, which seemed like a good idea at the time. I don't know what I was going to do with it, but I was angry, you get that right?"

"Ethan—"

"Then I stood outside his apartment, the one he kept so he had his single life, because I wouldn't do anything to him in front of his wife, it's not her fault. In fact, she seemed as if she might be a very nice lady when I spoke to her on the phone, and I—"

Jared shook his friend to stop the verbal diarrhea. "Ethan, breathe... and stay on topic."

"Oh, Marcus called the cops, but one of his neighbors turned up, Officer Lester, and there was an altercation, a scuffle if you will, and bang." He couldn't make a *bang* motion with his hands, so he replaced it with a heavy shrug and a little jump.

"'Bang.'"

"The device had a premature explosion, all over the officer, and of course, Marcus' fancy car." He bit his lip. "Marcus was more worried about his car than me. That's not right."

"Come on, let's get a cab."

"Can we afford that?" Ethan asked, and glanced up and down the street with concern.

"Yes, Ethan, we can."

Ethan was quiet on the way home, lost in thought, and Jared had learned there was only one way to get Ethan out of his spiral of thoughts, and that was to change the subject well away from Ethan's married boyfriend and purple dye all over said boyfriend's expensive car, not to mention Officer Lester.

"So I went to a bar to see the dad of that kid I found."

Jared waited for the words to compute, and then Ethan turned from staring out of the window and faced Jared in the dark interior.

"The kid?"

"You know, the one I told you about, on the steps outside work."

"Oh, yes, I remember the kid, a boy, right?"

"Luka, and he has a dad."

"Biologically, we all have dads." Ethan grinned, because to him that was a cool joke.

Jared ignored him, because that was the only way to

keep him on task and to forestall any more jokes in the same vein. "The dad owns a bar, Rhea's Bar, and I went there for a drink, and we sat and talked for a long time."

"Is he married?" Ethan's smile dropped.

"No, Nate's wife died, so he's a widower and a dad."

"Wow, that's a lot of stuff to unpack." Ethan patted his knee. "Sorry."

"Huh? Sorry for what?"

The cab had stopped on a red and streetlights illuminated the interior of the car, and Jared could see Ethan appeared sad. "Sorry for whatever has you telling me a sad story about a date with a dad who has a son. Surely it didn't end well."

"It was great, and it wasn't a date."

"You had drinks."

"Did you miss the part where he has a bar?" Jared was used to these conversations with Ethan that went off on tangents no one could follow, not even him, and he'd lived with Ethan for three years now.

"Oh, yes, a bar is certainly part of the equation, but you *had* drinks with him which has a very different connotation."

"I did." Jared sat back in his seat as the car moved again, knowing they were only a few minutes from home.

"Was it good?"

That was a loaded question. Jared had never felt so settled and happy than when he'd been sitting next to Nate talking about percentages and orders. Even now he could remember the scent of him as they leaned close, a mix of alcohol and whatever shower gel he'd used that smelled faintly of lemon. Or maybe it was polish from the bar. Whatever. All Jared knew was that Nate smelled wonderful, and was warm, and had a smile that lit him up from inside, and that Jared wanted to see him again.

"It was fun," Jared offered after a while, but something in his words, or his tone, or maybe in the way he was sitting, and Ethan was on him like a pack of starving wolves on fresh meat.

"Oh my god, you *like* like him," he announced and slapped a purple hand on Jared's knee. "Tell me everything. He's tall with dark hair, right? I know you like dark hair, and I bet his eyes are all shiny-bright, and he has a body to die for."

Jared knew better than to ask him how Ethan had deduced all that, because Jared had a type, and it was tall, dark, and sexy, much as Nate was.

"I do like him."

The cab pulled up outside their apartment and they slogged up the stairs to the fourth floor, and only when in the apartment, did Ethan curl up in the corner of the sofa and demand to know everything.

Jared told him what he felt he could, leaving out the fact that Luka was under the impression that he'd hired Jared, because it meant nothing. There was no way that Jared was staying away from Nate now, because after the drinks and the smiles and the laughing, whatever the barrier, Jared was intrigued and lusting after the gentle barman with sadness in his dark gaze, and bruises of exhaustion under his eyes. There was so much Jared wanted to know about Nate, what his hopes were for Luka's future, what kind of dad he was, right down to what his favorite food was for when Jared took him on a date. So many times as they'd sat working Jared had fought the instinct to touch Nate, not to mention kiss him. It seemed to Jared that Nate needed to be kissed, and Jared very much wanted to be the person to do that.

"You're really interested in this guy, aren't you." Ethan reached out and traced the purple handprint on Jared's jeans.

Jared grinned and settled back in his own corner of the beaten-up sofa.

"I'm going to go see him again, at the bar, ask him and Luka out for dinner."

"Him *and* Luka, eh?" Ethan gave him a knowing glance and Jared didn't look away.

All he knew is that he was excited to ask them both.

After I get some more sleep.

Chapter Eight

"Have you got your toothbrush?" Nate called to Luka.

"Yes," Luka shouted back.

"Clean underwear?"

"Dad," he whined and appeared in the doorway to Nate's bedroom. He shook his head. "Stop checking."

"Do you have everything for school tomorrow?" he pressed, having already buzzed Pops into the building.

Luka pulled a face. "Yes."

Nate chuckled. "Come here." He wrapped Luka in a hug. "You promise to be good for your grandma and grandpa?"

"I'm always good." Luka hugged Nate's waist. "Nana Kay said we're going to bake cookies."

"Cookies sound amazing." Nate rested his hand on Luka's head. "Save me some?"

Luka leaned back and looked thoughtful. "I don't know."

"You don't know?" Nate quirked an eyebrow. "You're breaking my heart."

"You said I shouldn't lie. What if they're really tasty and Pops eats them all?"

"Oh, Pops might eat them all?"

Luka grinned.

There was a knock at the door.

"That'll be your grandpa. Go check your things one last time."

"But Dad—"

"Do it," Nate said. He twisted Luka so he faced the opposite direction and gently pushed his back. "For me," he added.

"Fine." Luka slumped forward and swung his arms as he stomped back to his room.

Nate went to the door.

"Evenin'," Pops said, hunching in his thick coat. "Is Luka ready?"

"Come in. He won't be long."

Pops rubbed his hands together, stepped inside, and pushed the door shut behind him.

"Thanks for having him tonight."

"We love him staying over, you know that." Pops smiled.

"I know," Nate said, he glanced over his shoulder at the open door to Luka's room. "Luka, are you nearly ready?" Nate folded his arms, meeting Pops' gaze. "Also, I wanted to thank you for the hours you've been doing at the bar. It's really helped."

It was only two- or three-hour shifts here and there, but it was time Nate could make use of elsewhere, which then meant more time to focus on Luka as well.

"Here." Luka was in the hallway, wearing his coat,

beanie, and gloves. His rucksack was over his shoulder and he held an overnight carryall.

"Are you staying for a night or a week?" Pops teased and took the bag. "Geez, what have you got in here?" He lurched forward. "I'm kidding," he said when Luka frowned at him. "Come on. Your dad needs to get ready for work."

"Will Jared be there?" Luka asked.

"Jared? Why do you ask?"

"I don't know." Luka shrugged. "You gave him my letter and he…" He sighed. "Whatever."

Nate opened his mouth, stared at his son. "Why are you so interested in Jared?" It wasn't strange for Luka to get attached to people, but to do so after a single encounter seemed sudden. "Luka?"

"He helped me was all. I thought he was nice."

"Your dad thinks so, too." Pops rested a hand on Nate's shoulder. "Don't you?"

Nate glanced at Pops, then back at Luka who had his head down and wore a hurt expression.

Crap. What was my tone just now?

"Of course, I do." He relaxed his shoulders when Pops stepped back. It was as if his brain had stopped working where Jared was concerned. Despite his insistence the only important person he needed in his life was Luka, Nate's thoughts had turned to Jared on numerous occasions since his visit to Rhea's last week. Spending time with Jared had been comfortable and yes, he was nice, and maybe they could be friends.

Maybe. But they lived in different worlds. Jared was a university student, though a little late to it, he had aspirations, dreams, a future. What did Nate have to offer to a friendship, let alone anything else? He was an overworked single dad, a widower, someone scared to put himself out there for fear he, or worse, Luka, were to lose someone again.

He crouched in front of Luka and smiled. "When did you get so big?" He looked up at Luka. "If he comes again, I'll make sure I'm nice to him too." He tugged on Luka's sleeves then stood. "And I promise, if he does, I'll say hello from you."

A small smile twitched the corners of Luka's mouth. "Really?"

"Yes, really." He glanced at Pops. "Now, we've kept your grandma waiting long enough. You've cookies to bake, yeah?"

Luka nodded.

Pops put an arm around his shoulder. "Come on, kiddo," he said and hugged Luka to his side. "Let's leave your dad to his work."

"Love you," Nate said as they stepped outside. "I'll see you tomorrow." He waved, watched them to the stairs before closing the door.

When he was alone. Nate stood for a moment. The apartment felt different.

Silent. Empty. Cold.

Was Luka happy here? Comfortable? Was it still the warm and loving home it used to be?

What he thought of this place, his wants, needs, it didn't matter. He only ever wanted to see Luka smile.

That was enough.

. . .

"Have you had fun today?" Nate gripped his phone and leaned back in his office chair. He closed his eyes, listened to Luka and the sound of a barking dog in the background.

"Monty, down." Luka giggled, the volume of his voice rising and dropping as he moved about. "It's not for you."

"Everything okay?"

"He wants my cookie."

"Cookie? I thought it was bedtime."

Luka fell silent.

"Well, whatever." Nate sat forward. "My break's nearly up so I guess I'll say goodnight. Have a good day at school and I'll see you when you get home."

"Okay," Luka said. "Night-night. Bye."

There was the sound of rustling, then Kay spoke. "Hi, it's me again. He's on his way to bed so don't worry."

Nate laughed. "I'm never worried. Not when he's with you."

"Thank you."

"I should get back to work. But thanks for everything."

"It's fine anytime, you know that. You should come around soon. I don't feel like I've really seen you since Christmas."

"Sorry," Nate said.

"Oh, shush. I know you've a lot going on. Pops has been singing your praises, by the way. You, your staff, and your bar. I'm not sure he'd admit it but he's really enjoying the work. So, thank you."

"It's me who should be saying thanks."

"I'm pretty sure you already have. Several times." She gave a light laugh. "I should let you go. Take care, sweetheart."

"Thanks. You, too. Give him a big hug from me."

"Always do," Kay said. "Bye."

"Bye."

Nate hung up and placed his phone on the desk. He watched as the screen faded then turned off. He sighed, flinching when there was a knock on the office door. "Yes?" he called.

The door opened and Abi leaned inside. "It was quiet, so I figured you were done with your call."

"I was saying goodnight to Luka."

"I know. You always do when you're here late." Abi smiled.

Nate cleared his throat. "Did you need me for something?"

"Oh, right." She raised her tattooed hands in front of her, as if she had forgotten her reason for being there. "There's a guy asking for you."

"A guy? Who? He got a name."

"Jared something. He's kinda cute and charming. Is he your… are you and him…"

Nate frowned as he realized what she was getting at. "No. He's just a friend." Though exactly what he meant by calling Jared his friend was still a little unclear.

"Huh. I see. Well, he asked if you were in tonight. I told him you were and would let you know. Hope that was okay." She curled her lips then flashed her gritted teeth as she wore an awkward expression.

"It's fine. As I said, he's a friend. If you haven't already, get him a drink and tell him I'll be out in a minute."

Abi raised her hand, offered him a salute. "Will do, boss." She grinned, pulling the door closed as she left.

Nate sat back and laid a hand over his stomach. An unexpected mix of excitement and relief tumbled within him. Things had been piling up—stress of work, worry about Luka, the apartment, bills, everything. All meaning he was yet again neglecting his own feelings and needs.

My feelings? He wasn't sure he understood them or himself anymore. Rhea had. It was as if a simple smile from her could cast a spell and make everything right. She had known what he needed before he knew himself. Always.

Sitting here isn't going to achieve anything. It was better when he was busy. Sure, running the bar was hard and tiring but anything was better than an empty room and silence, just him and his thoughts. He grabbed his phone and left the office.

"Nate. Good evening," Jared said with a short wave. He was perched on a stool at the bar, a bottle of beer in front of him. He smiled brightly and Nate could have been fooled into thinking everything was going to be okay. Jared's smile wasn't the same as Rhea's, didn't weave the same magic, but he had to admit it helped. He didn't feel as alone as he had before.

Stupid, he chided himself. What was he even thinking?

"Hey, Abi said you were here. Just passing through?"

Jared shook his head. "I came to see you."

Nate's heart leapt, and for the briefest of moments he was happy. He swallowed hard as his chest tightened and thumbed the back of his wedding band as guilt crept in—guilt for the fleeting happiness that had bubbled to the surface.

"Nate?" Jared leaned forward, slid his hand across the bar in Nate's direction. "Are you okay?"

"I am," Nate insisted. "It's just been a weird, long day."

"Weird how?" Jared's expression was one of innocent curiosity.

Nate blew out a breath. "I don't know really. Guess I'm getting hung up on things I should have figured out by now. Don't tell anyone, but I'm a terrible grownup sometimes." He quirked an eyebrow. "Wait. Is this you trying to psychoanalyze me or whatever you call it?"

Jared shook his head. "No. This is me trying to be a friend. I know you wouldn't think it to look at me, but you should probably know, I have my moments of being a terrible grownup, too."

"You're just saying that to make me feel better."

"I'm not. You should ask my boss. I'm surprised I've not been fired." He gave an awkward laugh, his mouth twitching before he looked away.

"You said you worked part-time as well as being a student, but I'm not sure you ever said what you do."

"Didn't I?" Jared pursed his lips.

"If you did, I don't remember." It wasn't hard to believe he'd forgotten with everything going on with Luka. "So, what do you do, for work?"

Jared shrugged. "Lots of things."

Nate leaned his head to one side, stared at Jared.

"That makes it sound like I do something shady, doesn't it?"

"A little."

Jared laughed. "It's a hire company. It provides staff for events and stuff. Temporary gigs."

Nate wasn't sure he completely understood. "So, staff for catered events? That type of thing?"

"Yes, kind of. But it's not all that interesting." Jared took a drink of his beer. "I just go where I'm told to. Do what needs doing."

"I don't believe you." Nate crossed his arms.

Jared froze. "Which part?"

"About doing as you're told. Because if you did, then why would you think they'd fire you?" He pursed his lips. When was the last time he'd teased someone other than Luka?

"Ah, I did say that didn't I."

"You did."

Jared downed what was left of his beer. "There may have been a few mistakes along the way. But I swear, they're always done with the best of intentions. I'm just too nice. Or so people keep telling me." He chuckled and turned the empty bottle so the label was facing Nate.

Nice, huh?

"I guess you are." Nate glanced along the bar to where Abi was serving a group. He turned back and met Jared's eyes. "But I wouldn't say it's a bad thing."

"Exactly. I didn't think so either. But again, probably

not what my boss would say. There was this whole thing with a swan."

"Should I even ask?"

"Best if you don't." He grinned.

"Just answer me one thing. Is the swan okay?"

"Yeah. Or at least it was as I watched it waddle into the sunset with a hotel guest's shoe gripped firmly in its beak."

"Shoe? So many questions."

Laughing, Jared rested his folded arms on the edge of the bar. "Speaking of questions. I had one for you."

"Really?"

Jared nodded.

"Okay. Go on."

"I wanted to invite you out for dinner. You and Luka," he quickly added.

"Both of us?"

"Yeah. I wanted to talk to you some more, get to know you, as friends, and well, Luka's a big part of that. But if you think that's too weird, then…"

Nate narrowed his eyes. He studied Jared, his expression, his body language. Was this him being *too* nice? "It's not weird. I'm surprised, that's all." Even if Nate had been willing to open his heart to any of the men he had slept with since Rhea, he was sure very few would have stuck around for long. He didn't want to call Luka baggage, but that's what he would have been seen as.

"Then, what do you think? Would you like to? We could get burgers again, or is there somewhere Luka enjoys going?"

Somewhere Luka enjoys?

"You really are a nice guy."

"Huh?"

"Nothing." He clenched his fists, noting the feel of his ring between his tensed fingers. There were things he regretted about the past. Moments he should have acted upon. Hindsight was a bitch.

"So, dinner?"

"On one condition."

Jared sucked on his teeth. "Which is?"

"Instead of going out, let me cook."

"Are you sure you're okay with that?"

"In what way?"

"It's your home. Are you sure it's okay for me to be there?"

Nate dismissed Jared's concerns. "Why wouldn't it be? I'm inviting a friend over for dinner." He relaxed his arms at his side. "You wanted to get to know me and Luka better. This way you can. But if you don't feel comfortable—"

"I'll come," Jared interrupted. "I didn't want you to feel you had to invite me, is all. But I want to have dinner with you both."

Would Luka smile when Nate told him?

Nate's lips twitched.

Was it okay for him to smile, too?

"Are you free Sunday evening? Around five."

Jared took a moment, but eventually agreed. "Sure."

"Is there anything you don't eat? Allergies or anything?"

Jared shook his head. "None that I know of."

"Great. So, Sunday at five."

"Yes. Do you want me to bring anything with me?"

"Other than an empty stomach, I don't think so."

"I can do that," Jared said.

"Great," Nate said again. It was then panic started to set in. When was the last time he'd cooked for someone else? Luka was a child, easy to impress, easy to please. "Okay, I'm going to put this out there. Please don't go expecting some five-star dining when you come over."

"I won't."

"I'm not saying I'm bad. I'm not going to poison you or anything, but I'm completely average when it comes to the kitchen. I mean it's totally edible and—"

"It'll be fine." Jared's words helped ease Nate's anxiety. "I'm good with anything."

"Really?"

Jared rested his elbows on the bar. His cheeks puffing a little he held his head in his hands and met Nate's eyes. He gave a warm smile as he said, "Really."

Nate returned his smile. Heat spread through his body as he held Jared's gaze, and for the first time in a long time, there was something to look forward to.

I wish it was already Sunday.

Chapter Nine

Jared was never happier to see the back of a Saturday. He'd spent from six a.m. right up until eleven at night studying until his eyes crossed, broken only by Ethan forcing snacks into his hand and demanding he eat and drink. By the time he'd fallen into bed he was convinced he was going to forget everything he'd learned. Exams loomed, and if he didn't pass them then he was fucked, and not the good kind of fucked.

There was no way he wasn't going to pass, even if it meant putting in more days like yesterday, just as long as he didn't miss out on down time and in particular, one thing that had kept him going all week—dinner with Nate and Luka. He'd studied until three, and then he gave himself a full hour to get ready to head out. Like him and Ethan, Nate and Luka lived in Queens, but that was where the similarity ended. Nate had a place in Bay Ridge, a more family oriented place that had way lower rents than near the bar but was still more expensive than where Jared and Ethan lived. He didn't know the address and had to look it up to check he left with time to spare. His first idea was to walk the twelve blocks to Nate's place, but that meant less time to study, so a cab it was. He could always walk home.

After the shower he then had to decide what to wear. He hadn't had this much trouble since his senior prom, and his forays out to the living room where Ethan nursed a soda as he watched a documentary about meerkats, were getting more erratic.

"You're sure about the red."

"Yes, Jared, I'm sure about the red."

"But the blue—"

"If you ask me one more time for my opinion I will be forced to lock you out of your bedroom so you can't spend any more time in the closet." Ethan chuckled. "See what I did there?"

"Ha freaking ha, asshole."

"I'm the asshole? It's not *me* who keeps interrupting *me* and my weekly Discovery catchup. Anyway," he lifted his laptop, "I have work, so can you be quieter with your whole diva breakdown?"

Jared sighed heavily and padded back to his open closet, eyeing the complete destruction of his once organized room—books and study material, and clothes strewn across the floor. At least he hadn't touched his rent-a-boyfriend clothes. These were fancy tuxes and suits that Bryant & Waites supplied him with, and the latest one had arrived yesterday, all ready for the next booking, which would refill his waning pot of cash.

As long as I don't lose my shit and mess it up.

He did one last turn in front of the full-length

mirror. Nice jeans that showed off his ass, check. Clean scarlet T-shirt without a single crease, check. Clean-shaven with no cuts, nicks, or missed bits. Check, check and check.

Jacket on, he grabbed his wallet, noogied Ethan on his way past, only just escaping as his roommate tried to catch him to get him back, and then he slipped on his coat at the door, pocketed his keys and thought about what he might have forgotten.

"It's on the counter," Ethan called.

"What?"

"The wine you were just about to forget, idiot!"

Jared rolled his eyes at himself. He got the wine and did one more run through. Tonight was a big night in more ways than one. He wanted to get to know Nate and Luka, and much like the meerkats on the television right now, he was desperate to learn about the family dynamics. Luka clearly adored his dad, enough to think of hiring him a friend. Luka was smart, funny, sweet, and just the right mix of naive and super smart, which Jared loved in his nieces and nephews. Jared's siblings called him a big kid, and maybe they were right because he really felt a connection to Luka. Then there was Nate. Big, strong, sexy, vulnerable, dark-eyed Nate with the weight of the world on his shoulders, and his cautious smile.

Tonight Jared wanted to see a smile with no worries lurking in the shadows, to see Nate with his defenses lowered.

He also hoped he'd get to spend some time with

Nate on his own, a glass of wine, good food, maybe even a kiss.

Kissing Nate was his current obsession and the first thing that slipped into his mind in between writing essays and reading notes.

"You forgot the ice cream," Ethan added when Jared opened the front door.

Fuck my life.

The chocolate ice cream bought especially for Luka because he'd loved it at the restaurant. Jared had gone out of his way, made a trip to Van Leeuwen's just to get the best he could, and had a tub of it in the small freezer. He took out the ice cream, pushed it into his backpack and that was it, nothing else to delay him, so job done—he called out a thank-you to Ethan then headed downstairs, hailing a cab. The journey wasn't long, but it gave him a chance to calm down from the whole what-he-should-wear debacle, and by the time the cab stopped outside the apartment block they lived in, he was just leveled out at excited.

He pressed the button to get buzzed in, a disembodied voice telling him to come right up, and he headed up to the third floor, the door already open and Luka waiting for him, a wide grin on his face.

"Dad burned the 'sagna, but it was okay," Luka announced, and held out his hand palm up, some coins sitting there. "For tonight," he added under his breath.

"I didn't burn it," Nate called from somewhere inside. "It's crispy! And let him in Luka."

Jared didn't want the coins, but Luka thrust them at him and almost dropped them as he did.

"Luka, you don't need to—"

"Jared! Hey." Nate appeared behind his son, and Jared smoothly pocketed the coins. Nate was a sight for sore eyes, dark jeans, a grey sweater with a lighter thread in it, his hair still damp, and a dishtowel over his shoulder.

"Hi." Jared didn't know what else to say or do, because all he could think was how had he forgotten every detail of Nate so badly to now be struck dumb. Was he supposed to shake Nate's hand, or hug him, or maybe push him against the nearest wall and kiss the life out of him? Scratch that, the last thing was not on the agenda.

"Come in. Luka, let Jared in."

Jared shrugged off his backpack and out of his coat, adding it to the ones on the hooks inside the small entry hall. Right next to the coats was a corkboard, and it had a load of notes posted and a calendar with days colored in with different highlighters. Nate must have noticed Jared glancing at it because he pulled Luka in for a side hug and huffed a laugh.

"We live a complicated life," he explained.

"I wasn't... I didn't mean to... I brought wine." It wasn't like him to trip over his words, but Nate smelled so good, if a little smoky, and Luka was staring up at him expectantly. "And this is for you." He passed the tub of ice-cream to Luka.

"All for me?" Luka asked with wide eyes.

"Yeah."

"I'mma getting a spoon," he announced, but Nate

beat him too it, grabbing the tub and holding it high and out of Luka's reach.

"After dinner," he announced with a secret smile.

"But you burned dinner," Luka whined.

"I did not burn it, as I said, it's just a little crispy and I got rid of the bit that was uhmm... too crispy."

"Burned," Luka muttered under his breath, then headed through another door and into a wide open living space.

"Make yourself at home and I'll get a glass." He gestured with the wine.

Jared didn't follow him out of the main room, he hadn't been asked to... Maybe Nate didn't want to share the origin of the burning incident. So, Jared stayed where he was and Luka immediately started giving him a guided tour, which consisted of him pointing out the sofa, the window, the TV, and his room. As he was tugged around he noticed just how many photos were on display—they were everywhere, cataloguing every single stage of Luka's life from baby to what seemed like recent shots, and in the corner, right by the door to Luka's bedroom, there was a photo of Nate, his arms around a heavily pregnant woman.

"That's my mom. She was called Rhea, like the bar," Luka said.

"I remember your dad said that. You look a lot like her," Jared observed, and he wasn't lying. Even though Luka was a mini-Nate in a lot of ways, he could see Rhea's beautiful smile in Luka.

"She was very pretty."

"She was beautiful."

"She was," Nate said from behind them, and Jared turned to face him, feeling guilty for having been staring at Rhea. "She had a beautiful soul, and we miss her."

Jared examined Nate's expression, a hazard of his studies, and yes he saw grief, but he also saw pride. He wanted to say something profound, but he didn't get the chance because Nate smiled at him and offered a glass.

"Nice wine," he murmured and took a sip. "I don't get to drink much wine, just a ton of spirits." He shook his head. "I sound like an alcoholic."

"I knew what you meant."

"I need to write about chickens," Luka announced, "can I go finish my homework?" He blinked at his dad so innocently, but Jared got the feeling that he was just giving his dad alone time to be with his new friend. He bet it never occurred to Luka that Jared wanted to kiss Nate though, or be more than friends. Maybe even boyfriends? That was a bridge they would cross when they got to it—if he and Nate got to it.

"Hang on bud, you're voluntarily going to do homework?" Nate touched Luka's forehead. "Are you feeling okay?"

If looks could kill, then Nate would've been on the floor, not breathing, but when Luka flounced off with a muttered something or other Nate was grinning, and the love for his son was front and center.

"So, how's the bar?" Jared began the one conversation he knew would carry on and maybe lead into other things, because he couldn't think of anything else.

"The suppliers liked the report and they put me up a level in approved discounts."

"That's cool."

"And college?" It was Nate's turn to cover the basics.

"Too much studying, too much debt," Jared quipped.

Then they stared at each other, and Jared considered what it would be like to step into Nate's space and kiss him. For the longest moment he wondered if maybe Nate was thinking the same thing, and then he cleared his throat and went through the door to the kitchen.

"Hungry?" he asked over his shoulder, and Jared followed him, not into a scene of chaos with burned lasagna and dishes everywhere, but to an oasis of calm. "Sorry about the table, it was Luka's idea, and he's already eaten a whole pile of what he calls burned lasagna, so it's just us."

Jared hadn't even noticed the tiny table tucked into the corner, laid with placemats and hand-drawn name plates, and in the center a vase filled with paper flowers, but now he'd seen it he couldn't un-see it.

Because to him it was as if Luka had set it for a romantic dinner.

So maybe Jared didn't need to worry about what Luka thought about him kissing Nate at all.

Chapter Ten

What's with this setup?

Nate sipped his wine, eying the small bunch of paper roses Luka had tricked him into making with him earlier that afternoon.

"I want to give them as a present to Lee," Luka had said.

When Luka had asked for a vase, Nate had thought nothing of it. It wasn't until he'd walked into the kitchen and found Luka fussing over the table settings that he pointed out the lie. In response, Luka had calmly said he hadn't lied. He would give them to Lee tomorrow, but they could be used as way of a table decoration in the meantime.

He glanced at Jared opposite him. It was the two of them.

Why is it only the two of us?

The scene was too intimate. Too much just Jared and him. Alone. Together. This wasn't the plan. Luka had been talking about Jared and dinner on and off all weekend and now Jared was here, Luka had dipped.

Without a single prompt from Nate, he had taken himself away to finish homework that wasn't due until the end of the week.

What was *that* about?

The meal was supposed to be for the three of them — Luka, him and Jared. A family dinner. A *friends* dinner? Whatever it was called, it was meant to be a meal for three. Nate felt cheated somehow. Conspired against.

Nate lowered his glass.

Sure, dinner might be a little awkward, a little too cozy. But it was what it was. They were here, together and as much as the thought of it being the two of them made Nate want to run, fling open Luka's bedroom door and drag him back to the table, he had to admit it wasn't completely terrible being only him and Jared. It was comfortable, relaxing, easy.

Should it be this easy being around somebody? Somebody like Jared?

"Don't force yourself," Nate said, breaking the silence they had fallen into between bites of dinner. He leaned back in his seat. "You don't have to finish it."

Jared met Nate's eyes over the fork full of food he held up. "Why wouldn't I?" Jared filled his mouth, chewed. He raised his hand, covering his lips as he mumbled, "It's good."

Nate chuckled. "Is this you being too nice right now?"

Jared shook his head. "Of course not. But you're acting like it's the worst lasagna ever made. You should try living at my place. I conveniently find myself having other plans when it's my roommate's turn to cook. That or suggest getting takeout."

"Worse than super crispy lasagna? I don't believe you."

"Okay so it's not *all* the time, but he sure has his moments. He's massacred everything from a side salad to steak to—"

"I love steak," Nate uttered.

Jared smiled. "Not so sure you'd be saying that if you saw Ethan's idea of a steak. I love the guy, but he'll try his hand at anything and has this habit of adding his own twists to recipes. I think it's the crazy scientist in him. He comes up with some odd creations and I swear given a chance he'd cook everything over a Bunsen burner." He raised his empty fork and pointed it in Nate's direction. "And anyway, quit it would you? The lasagna's not *super* crispy, just a little crunchy on the outside. It's fine once you rummage beneath the surface."

Nate raised an eyebrow. "Why does it sound like you're describing my father-in-law?"

"Huh?"

In a deep tone, Nate said, "Beneath his crunchy, tough exterior is a big old soft-hearted idiot. All meat and sauce." He twisted his wine glass on the table, remembered the almost theatrical performance Rhea had given when explaining Pops in advance of Nate meeting her parents for the first time. He chuckled, rubbed the crease at his brow. Maybe the wine was going to his head. "Ignore me."

"Do you get on with him? Your father-in-law? I met him at the bar the other night, didn't I?"

"Yes, that's him, Don, or rather, Pops. Everybody calls him Pops once they get to know him. He's a teddy bear really, always been this fatherly, lend his ear to anyone and their problems kind of guy, if you know what I mean."

"Ah, the clichéd role of a bartender."

Nate nodded. "Pretty much. It suits him, though. I have a barman, Gregg, who's similar. He's my second in command, the assistant manager." He drank the last of the wine in his glass. "He runs things when I'm at home with Luka."

"Must be good to have someone to rely on."

"I trust him. Or rather Rhea did. She hired him, must be six, seven years now. I'm glad he stuck around, though I sometimes wonder if he aspires to own a bar of his own someday." He sucked on his teeth. "I'm sure he said something like that in his interview."

"Where do you see yourself in ten years? That question?"

"Probably," Nate said with a chuckle. He stared at his empty glass. Where had Nate seen himself now, ten years ago? He was sure whatever he'd thought, Rhea had been part of it.

He tilted his empty glass. It wasn't a good idea to drink too much, especially if a single glass had his face feeling flushed and his thoughts lingering in the past. Luka had school in the morning, and Nate planned on sorting through some paperwork once Jared had gone and Luka was in bed.

"Dad," Luka stuck his head in the gap of the open door. He puffed his cheeks, pulled the door to him so his face was smushed between the door and the frame.

"Need some help?" Nate asked.

Luka shook his head and pushed open the door. "I'm done for today." He put his hands behind his back and eyed the dishes on the table.

"Do you want some more?"

Luka once again shook his head. "I was just looking."

"You lost something?" Jared glanced over his shoulder.

Luka stepped forward. "Nope." He smiled at Nate.

"Oh, I see. Somebody wants that ice cream." Nate waggled his finger, indicating for Luka to come to him. He hooked his arm around Luka's waist. "How about you help me get started on clearing up, and when Jared's ready and everything's tidy, we can all sit down with big bowls of ice cream."

Luka squirmed when Nate pinched his side. "Can we watch a movie?"

"Um. We could, but Jared will probably have to go home before it finishes, and I'd hate for him to miss the end." He looked at Jared. "I mean, you're welcome to stay if you wanted to. Just, I'm sure you've better things to do with your evening."

Jared placed his cutlery on his empty plate and wiped his hands on his napkin. "I've no plans so I can do whatever. It's fine if you want to kick me out though."

"There's no rush." Nate released Luka and slid back his chair.

"Can I give you a hand?" Jared asked as he held out his plate.

"No need. Luka and I have got this." He took the plate. "But if you want to help, you can grab the ice cream from the freezer. And bowls and spoons. They're in the middle cabinet and top drawer on the left. Okay?"

"Spoons, bowls, and ice cream. I can do that."

"Come on," Nate said to Luka. "Let's clear the dirty dishes."

It didn't take long to wash and dry the handful of dishes and put away the leftovers. And then, each with a bowl of chocolate ice cream in hand, they headed for the living room. Luka darted in front of them, grabbing the remotes from the coffee table then laying claim to and curling up on the single armchair, leaving Nate and Jared to take the couch.

With a sigh, Nate pressed down the ice cream as it melted. He raised his shoulders. He felt as if someone were watching him. He turned his head to find Jared grinning at him. "What?"

Jared stirred his spoon. "Always got told by my brothers I was weird for pretty much turning my ice cream into an extra thick milkshake any time we had it at home."

Nate stared down at the creamy goop swirled in the bottom of his dish. He cleared his throat. "Rhea used to…" He checked on Luka who was engrossed in some animated movie he'd chosen. "And then she did it for Luka and I guess I got in the habit, too." He picked up his spoon and filled his mouth with the lumpy cold paste. He licked his lips. The chocolate was sweeter than he'd thought it was going to be. "It's good," he said, hoping to keep the conversation from settling on the past. "Thank you for bringing it."

"No worries." Jared licked the ice-cream from his spoon and Nate couldn't help but let his gaze linger on Jared's mouth, the way his lips curled around the spoon, and the flick of his tongue.

What the hell am I thinking?

When Jared focused on the TV, Nate was left feeling relieved.

The movie played out over the next eighty minutes. A group of children helping a large fluffy creature find its way home. Nate breathed in as the credits rolled and exhaled out of his nose when he spotted Luka draped over the arm of the chair, his eyes closed.

"Lightweight," Jared said in a low voice and smiled.

Nate stretched back his shoulders then got to his feet. "Think he was a bit too excited about you coming over."

He was aware neither him nor Luka had slept well the last two nights. Excitement and joy, fear and doubt. Lots of feelings had stirred inside Nate about inviting Jared into his home.

He crouched down, looking at his openmouthed son. "Hey, Luka." He gently prodded Luka's cheek. "Luka."

Luka groaned and his eyelids fluttered as he woke. He rolled his head. "Huh? Dad? Ten more minutes."

Nate sighed. "It's time for bed not school. Come on. Get up."

Luka licked his lips. Brown chocolatey stains were in the corners of his mouth. He opened his eyes wider and arched his neck. "Jared's still here." He sounded a mix of surprised and relieved.

Jared gave him a little wave.

"He is, so come and say goodnight. And make sure to thank him again for the ice cream."

Luka rolled himself off the chair and landed on his knees on the floor. He stretched his arms above his head, then pulled himself to his feet using the side of the armchair. He went to Jared's side.

Nate collected the bowls from the coffee table. "Make it quick, then straight to bed. And make sure you wash your mouth properly." He left Luka to his goodbyes and took the dishes through to the kitchen. He placed them by the sink and rubbed the back of his neck. It was already after eight.

"Need any help?" Jared asked from behind him, startling him.

"Jeez." Nate turned to face him and leaned back against the edge of the counter.

"Sorry. Did I scare you?"

Nate shook his head. "Not really. I was just… I don't know. Mind wandered I guess."

"Luka's gone to brush his teeth."

"Right." Nate turned around and turned on the faucet, held his hand under the water waiting for it to run warm. "Sorry if you were bored. It's been a while since we had guests over."

"It was fine."

"Luka was happy you came." He glanced over his shoulder. Jared had stepped farther into the room.

"He was?"

Nate nodded. He focused on rinsing out the bowls. "Yeah. I don't know why."

"Harsh," Jared said.

Laughing, Nate piled the dishes and turned off the water. "You know I didn't mean it that way." He turned around. Jared had moved even closer and the expression he wore made Nate uneasy.

The way he's looking at me.

It was then Jared asked, "And you?" He ran his hand over the countertop as he took a step. "Were you happy I came?"

Was I?

An ache spread in his chest and it had nothing to do with burned lasagna or feasting on rich ice cream. It hurt and yet, he welcomed the familiar sensation as it spread lower.

Attraction? Desire? Want? It was seeped in the weight of emotions. Looking at Jared, just hanging out with him, those moments had brought feelings to the surface he hadn't felt or wanted to feel in a long time. His fleeting nights with men like Michael were about escaping. There were no feelings, no connections, and yet with Jared, there was something about him that stirred up Nate's insides the more time he spent with him.

It's scary.

"I—"

"Dad!" Luka's footsteps grew louder as he ran to the kitchen. He jumped through the door, announcing, "All done." He was already in his pajamas.

Nate cleared his throat. Reset his focus. "Let me see."

Luka grumbled but walked over to him, leaned his head back, and beamed up at him.

"Ah, yes. All clean," Nate noted. "Go on. I'll see you to bed." He walked past Jared. "If you want to finish the wine or want anything else to eat just help yourself. I'll be back in a minute."

"Sure. Night, Luka."

"Night," Luka said cheerily.

Nate rested his hand on Luka's back and guided him out of the kitchen and to his bedroom.

"Is Jared going home now?" Luka asked as he enacted his usual routine of throwing soft toys to the floor and scrambling in a circle until he slid beneath the covers.

"He will be in a little while. I'm sure he has school tomorrow, just like you." Nate planted a kiss on his head. "So, straight to sleep. Okay?"

Luka wriggled under the cover. "Yep."

"Goodnight." Nate backed out of the room, flicking the light switch as he went and pulling Luka's door closed, leaving a crack for the light from the hallway to filter in. He stared back at the kitchen door. "Jared?" he said.

"In here," Jared said from the living room.

Nate found Jared, a glass of wine in his hand, standing on the far side in front of the large bookcase that filled half of the wall. He was leaning forward, eying the collection of photo frames. The lower two shelves used to house rows of well-thumbed books, their spines creased, corners tattered from numerous reads. Most had belonged to Rhea, a collection of light romance novels, easy reads she was happy to lose herself in again and again. It had been a week since he'd taken them off there, putting them in a box and sliding them into the bottom of his closet. He wasn't ready to get rid of them entirely, they were part of the tapestry that had been her. Luka might want them one day.

Why did I put them away? Why now?

He had refilled the shelves with framed photographs and various memories they had collected over the years as a family, and the ones of him and Luka since she'd been gone. One day there would be more photos of him and Luka alone than had ever been taken of them together when Rhea was alive.

He wasn't cutting her out of his life—he doubted that was ever possible, not when she was still in Luka's dark eyes, and still had a place in Nate's heart. But just for a moment, it was as if the veil of grief had lifted a tiny bit more and he was allowing sunshine in.

Jared and his smile. Maybe?

"She really was beautiful," Jared stated as Nate drew close. "You look happy together."

Nate stood beside him and gazed at the photographs. "We were."

"How long since…" He picked up one of the frames. In it was a picture from Nate and Rhea's wedding day.

"Four years."

"How did she… Sorry I shouldn't ask."

"It's okay. It was stupid bad luck mainly." He took the photo from Jared and smoothed a thumb over the picture. They'd been so happy on that day, full of excitement for the future, and in a second it had gone. "It was an aneurysm. One minute she was here and the next…" He passed the photo back to Jared who placed it carefully back on the shelf.

He had wanted to be able to make the most of his life in her memory. Do the things she couldn't, see things and places she would now never go. But he was finding it so hard—impossibly hard. He knew it was his fault, too consumed by the bar to give himself time to process, too worried about forgetting her to begin to look to the future, and too hung up on the past. Guilt flooded him whenever he thought about doing anything they'd spoken about when for her they were now impossible. He had to put everything he had into seeing their boy grew up happy and healthy.

But am I going about it the right way?

He spent as much time as he could with Luka while still working at the bar. He wanted to provide, to save up so Luka could go to college, just like Jared, so he could do anything he put his mind to.

"You're doing a good job, you know?" Jared said.

"Sorry?"

"With Luka."

"Sure," Nate said dismissively. Did Jared have superpowers after all?

Can he see inside my head?

"I mean it. Because you're wearing a rather incredible frown right now and I get the impression that's your 'Luka' face." Jared smiled.

Nate folded his arms across his chest. Jared wasn't wrong but still... "That's kind of creepy."

Jared snorted a laugh. "My bad. But I'm right, aren't I?"

Nate nodded. "I can't help worrying about him, and the bar, and the future, and the past. The woes of being a single working father I guess." He pursed his lips, narrowing his eyes as he studied the picture of Luka from a couple of years ago. "Am I really doing okay? Is Luka okay?"

"He's loved, looked after, and in the short amount of time I've known him, and you, I'd say he's a lucky kid, and a happy one."

Nate side-eyed Jared. "Everything looks better with a glass of wine in your hand."

"You need to stop and just take the compliment. I am a psychology student, remember. I know this stuff."

Nate worried his lower lip between his teeth. He wasn't going to win against Jared. He was sure of that. "Fine," he said. "And thank you." He met Jared's eyes. They were a soft hazel-green even in the soft glow of the ceiling lights. "I mean it."

Jared drained his glass and turned, leaning behind him to slip it onto the edge of the coffee table. When he stood back up, he had closed the gap between them. "You're welcome," he said. His gaze lingered on Nate's.

The moment they shared was heavy and Nate wished Jared would look away.

"You never answered my question before," Jared stated. A brightness danced in his eyes.

"Which question?" Nate asked, but he already knew what Jared meant.

Why did I ask? I don't want him to ask. If Jared repeated his question, then Nate would have to answer. There was no Luka to aid in his escape this time.

"Are you happy I came tonight?"

Ah, he said it.

Nate wanted to step back, but Jared kept drawing him in.

I should be honest.

"Yes," he said. "But…"

"But what?" Jared moved closer, tilting his head as he seemed determined to keep his eyes firmly locked with Nate's.

"I don't know." Nate wasn't sure what he was feeling. Yes, he was happy and yes, it was scary, but he didn't mind. In truth, being with Jared made some things less scary.

I'm contradicting myself. I'm so confused.

"Then how about I help you figure it out?"

"How…" His chest tightened as Jared leaned in.

He's going to kiss me. I should pull away, push him away. I should…

Jared stopped, his lips a breath away from Nate's as if waiting for Nate to stop him.

I want to. I don't want to.

Nate closed his eyes, went with the flow and leaned the final distance to the kiss. It was gentle, a lingering connection of their lips as Jared pressed his mouth to

Nate's. Nate swallowed hard, opened his eyes when the kiss ended, and Jared pulled back. A pain tightened his chest and he hugged himself, folding his arms across his stomach. This wasn't like the sex-driven hookups he'd had in the past, not random kissing for nothing but getting off, this was more—a promise of sorts, and it scared the life out of him.

"Are you okay?" Jared asked. "Sorry. Maybe I shouldn't have done that. I said we were friends and a friend... a friend shouldn't have done that."

Nate shook his head. "It's fine. You don't have to apologize."

I wanted you to kiss me. I let you.

He glanced at the bookcase, at the photographs, at Rhea. She was right there.

"I'll go." It was as if Jared knew the turmoil Nate had found himself in.

"You don't have to," Nate managed.

"I do." Jared stepped back. "And if you decide you don't want to see me anymore then that's okay. I get it."

I don't want that, but... Please go. I need to think.

Nate didn't say anything. He stared at the floor as he tried to wrestle with the contradictions that stabbed at him.

"It's not your fault. I kissed you so don't hate yourself. You didn't betray anyone." Jared left the room to where his coat was hanging in the hallway.

Why are you so understanding? How can you be so selfless?

Nate followed after him. What should he say?

Jared opened the apartment door.

"Jared," Nate said in a hushed voice. "I don't hate myself and I didn't hate…it. I just…"

"You need some time?" His smile was warm, understanding.

Nate nodded. "But, if you ever want to stop by the bar, for a cocktail, I wouldn't mind."

Jared ducked his head. "Thank you. I might just do that." He hesitated, finally saying, "Goodnight, Nate."

"Yeah, goodnight," he said, pushing the door closed once Jared had left.

It was then the sound of his heart beating filled the quiet apartment. Why did he feel more alone than ever? Why did he think that might be the last time he'd see Jared? What kind of catch was a man with one foot in the past?

For him, for Jared, for Luka. He needed to work out what he wanted, what the right thing to do was. He leaned back against the wall and closed his eyes as he touched his lips. Memories of the kiss lingered.

Could he *really* live the rest of his life without loving someone?

What should I do?

Chapter Eleven

Jared stayed away from Nate for two whole days. It wasn't a conscious decision to give Nate space, just that finals were looming, and he was determined to pass this exam with flying colors. His plans for the future depended on him passing with gold stars and fireworks, so he wouldn't be one of many who passed, but would stand out as the best damn psychology student the college had ever known.

Only tonight's studying was a bust.

He'd completed ten of the twelve courses, and was so close to completing the eleventh, but for some reason Theories of Personality was kicking his ass, and what he needed was a break. Nothing to do with the excitement in the pit of his stomach.

Who am I kidding? Any excuse to visit the bar is a good one.

He didn't have to analyze himself to know that he was desperate to see Nate again, only he had all the feels about how visiting now would be too soon. Nate was so unsure about the past, the future, whether or not he was a good dad, his bar, his wife, and Jared doubted Nate had made any kind of decision in two days about anything that he and Jared could do. Like kiss. Or date. Maybe he should ask Ethan if he wanted to go out, then it wouldn't be all Jared's fault if they ended up at Rhea's Bar.

"Do you want to go out?" he asked his roommate, who was poring over individual index cards he kept shuffling. "Ethan?"

"Hmmm?" Ethan murmured, and then in a flurry of movement he switched two of the cards and then stood back to examine him. This is how he worked, visually, messing with compounds and theories and concepts that somehow made sense to him.

"A drink? You want to get one?"

"Osmium!" Ethan announced with dramatic flair, then swept all the cards off the table and pulled out a new set of cards still in their cellophane. Jared watched him fumble at getting the plastic off the cards, and took it from him, pulling out the cards and handing them to Ethan who blinked at him like a newborn in daylight.

"That's a no on going out then."

Ethan blinked at him some more. "Osmium," he said, as if stating random elements made all the sense in the world.

"Definitely a no then." Jared patted his friend on the back as he backed away from the mad scientist in training. It seemed as if it was just him on his own, heading out for a drink with no purpose other than to get out of the apartment and burn off some angst over all the studying. And now he couldn't even blame Ethan.

So he'd find a local bar. The drink could be at any place—he didn't *have* to go to a place where Nate might be working. Even if he went to Rhea's, with its cozy atmosphere and its cocktails, that didn't mean that Nate would even be there at seven in the evening. He might be home with Luka, so what did it hurt to go to a bar he knew and liked? Somehow in all of that thinking, he'd concluded that it was fine to go to Rhea's Bar, and with that he grabbed his coat, keys, and wallet, and headed out. He chose to ignore that he'd pulled on his best jeans, changed into the softest T-shirt he owned, plus added the smartest button-down in his closet, shaved, styled his hair, and used cologne.

Just a normal everyday visit to any bar in New York.

Kind of.

He knew where he was going, because the thought of seeing Nate again made him smile, and he desperately wanted to just talk to him. Or kiss him. Or both.

He was disappointed not to see Nate behind the bar, instead he spotted Pops watching another guy who was mixing and muddling and doing whatever it took to create a cocktail. When the coolness of the city gusted in with Jared, he shut the door as Pops looked up, saw him, and then smiled in welcome.

"Just in time, kid!" he exclaimed, and gestured him over. "Jared, meet Gregg."

Gregg and Jared shook hands. This must be the Gregg who maybe wanted his own bar one day, and he did seem very proficient with the way he handled the bottles. "We're making… what's it called again, Gregg?"

"Rum Martinez—"

"Rum, maraschino liqueur, vermouth, but we don't have toasted wood chips or digital smoke infuser, so apparently it will never be as good as the original, but we could always rename it to like, I don't know, Rhea's Rum, or something. Let us know what you think."

"I actually came in to see—"

"Just a sip."

Jared did as he was asked, the smokiness of the mixed liquors hitting the back of his throat and filling his mouth with warmth. He was tempted to drink it all, but that wasn't how tastings worked, right?

"Really good," he summarized, then pushed the crystal tumbler back to Pops.

"Hmmm," Gregg murmured, and then traced his finger down a list on a sheet of paper. "Would you say that wood chips would make it more or less—"

"He won't know that," Pops interrupted Gregg who went back to his list. "I bet you're here to see Nate, right?"

"I was just going to get a drink," Jared lied.

Pops raised a single eyebrow in silent comment. "You just caught him, he's in the office but he's heading home soon," Pops explained all of that then topped it off with a smile and a wink and thumbed to the door in the corner. "He's been in there too long."

"Is it okay to just—"

"He's got his head in numbers, go rescue him." He slid the tumbler back, then pushed another toward Jared. "On the house, take this for Nate and ask him what he thinks, then tell him to go home. We got this."

Jared took the glass with him, heading around the bar, and knocking on the door, hearing a muffled *come in*, peeked inside. Nate's serious expression vanished in an instant, in fact it wasn't so much pleasure as utter relief.

"Since when did four plus four not equal eight?" he blurted, and Jared placed the cocktail in front of him.

"Pops said you need to try that," he lied. "And to tell you that you need to go home."

"I will as soon as I get this to balance."

"Give me the math."

He poked at his laptop, and then slid it over. "I swear numbers will be the end of me."

Jared only had to glance at the sheet he was working on to see where the error was. "You're rounding up or down all the way through so it's inevitable that you'll be out at the end, because you're adding up what's behind the numbers, not what you see on the screen."

Nate took a sip of the drink and looked at Jared with a blank expression. "Can you... magic..." He waved at the laptop, and Jared leaned over, followed the formulas back to the root of the issue, then a couple of changes later and everything added up. Not just that but Nate had finished his cocktail, staring at the empty glass as if it was going to bite him.

"That's good," he muttered, and then glanced up at Jared and gave him a shy smile. "Hi."

"Hi." Jared sat on the edge of the desk, crossing his legs at his ankles and sipping his drink.

"You're here."

"You sound shocked."

Nate sighed and shook his head. "You came over, we

watched a kids' movie and ate crispy lasagna, then I moped, the kiss was really quick, and I thought for sure I'd never see you again."

Jared counted the items on his fingers. "You didn't mope, I loved the movie, and the lasagna, and spending time with you and Luka." He put his empty glass down, then held out a hand, and after a moment's pause Nate took it and allowed himself to be tugged to his feet. "And the kiss was so perfect I'd like to do it again." Nate almost melted into him, but then he pulled back as if a thought suddenly occurred to him.

"I'm working for the next few nights, but after that, I made a decision that we should get dinner or something? Or not a decision, but there's a lot of things to think about, and I decided to ask you on a date... shit, I'm crap at this."

"A date would be good." Jared tugged a little more and Nate had to take a step forward to keep his balance. "There's this awesome diner I know that has these old-fashioned slot machines, give Luka a roll of quarters and he would love them."

"No, not with... not that I don't appreciate that you want to include Luka, because he's a really important part of my life, but... look, I'm messing this up. I meant just the two of us. Maybe?"

"You did?" Another tug and Nate was just one tiny step away, but even though Jared had thought of nothing else but kissing Nate again, the next move had to be on Nate. "Like a date for real?"

"We'd have to go later, or maybe Saturday, if I could get Pops to cover. Luka has been on his best behavior recently since… you know, so I agreed to let him go to a sleepover, and so I wouldn't have to worry about messing with Luka's weekend, because we have to get him new shoes, and somehow it's going to be a circus, because he hates shopping." He stopped talking. "Why am I even telling you that? My life is messy, but I wouldn't change it, only I don't know why you'd want to take this on, so maybe we shouldn't even start with a date, because one day you will—"

Jared pressed a finger to Nate's lips. Sunday, he had a job with a regular client, a last minute booking for a yachting event, or something to do with the docks and boats. To be honest he hadn't been listening to Rowan because he knew he'd get a file sent over in plenty of time and there was no way he could mess up a two-hour *date* where all he had to do was smile and act like a professional.

"Saturday is great. Although I can't stay long, I have work early on Sunday, and I'm knee-deep in exams."

"So Saturday it is, for dinner, just us." He seemed so focused, as if he'd made some huge decision and had found his resolve, or was that just wishful thinking on Jared's part?

"That sounds perfect."

Something changed in Nate's expression, focus replaced by unexpected determination. He moved closer, not completely trapping Jared against the desk, but when his tongue flicked out to wet his lips, it was obvious what he was asking. "I would really like to kiss you, again. This time for real."

Jared cradled Nate's face. "Sounds good."

Finally, Nate took that single move to bring them together and their lips met in a soft kiss. Once. Then again. The first time was quick, a test, the second lingered a bit longer, and it could have been more, but Nate pulled back. He pressed his hands to Jared's shoulders and held him still.

"It's important that I tell you, Luka will always come first."

"I know."

"And I'm not looking for a new mom or dad for Luka because the two of us are okay as we are."

Jared's chest hollowed at the pain in Nate's voice, but he tried very hard not to let Nate see his reaction. When he thought of Nate and Luka together he saw an impenetrable unit built on love, and he wasn't sure he'd ever be allowed inside, but right now he'd take every kiss he could get and be happy with it.

"It's just a kiss," Jared whispered. "I'm not looking to suddenly be Luka's dad, or your new start, I just think that kissing might be nice." *Nice* was underselling what he'd felt, because even the most chaste of kisses had sent shockwaves through his body, and not just because it was a wonderful kiss, but because Nate had lowered one of his barriers and let them try.

That was big.

"I want one more before I go home, and I really have to go home because I promised Luka a game of Jenga, and we're reading *The Hobbit*. The kids' version, with pictures, but we've just got to the troll bit and… yeah, I really want to go home."

Jared didn't miss the hint, kissing him before he

changed his mind, and both of them laughing into the kiss in their eagerness to get closer. He could stay here all night, taking his fill of Nate, but he hadn't missed the urgency in Nate's voice. When they parted it was Nate who chased for more, but he snapped out of it.

"I need to leave."

Jared wasn't ready for whatever this was to end, and they were, after all, heading vaguely in the same direction. "Me too," he lied, and quirked a smile, "we can go together."

Nate shrugged on his jacket and pulled a beanie down over his dark hair. "Let's go then."

They stood together on the platform as they waited for the next train. The wind was cold around them and they huddled closer until the train arrived and then darted on, huffing laughs as the door closed and they could work on getting warm. There were no seats, so they ended up moving through to stand and hold onto the bar, so close that Jared could've kissed Nate again.

Not the time or place. Not yet.

He didn't even kiss him when they reached Nate's stop and Nate whispered a goodbye.

"Saturday," he said instead.

"I suppose... did you want to come up?"

Oh god, he really wanted to go up, see Luka, play Jenga and listen to Jared read *The Hobbit*, but he instinctively understood that this would be the wrong kind of step to take.

"You have your evening planned, and I need to study, but say hi to Luka for me, and think about the diner with the slot machines, because it's fun and Luka would love it, yeah?"

Nate looked at him with a thoughtful expression. "I think you really mean it."

"Why wouldn't I? Luka's a good kid, fun, bright, just like all my nieces and nephews back home."

"You're a special kind of person, Jared." Nate lowered his head. Maybe he was just confused.

Jared attempted to lighten the moment. "Funny thing is, my family say I'm special as well, only not in a good way."

At last, with a smile on his face, Nate left, and Jared waited until the entry door shut behind him before leaving.

Then he walked home, counting down the hours until Saturday.

Chapter Twelve

"Hey, Nate. A hand. Please." Pops leaned from behind the stack of boxes he was carrying and stared at Nate.

Nate stared back. "Oh." He pocketed his cell. "Sorry," he said and took the top box. It was lighter than he had imagined. "What are these?" He slid the box onto the counter, tilting his head to read the contents.

"Chips," Pops said.

"Huh?"

"Gregg spoke to ya, right? About the new range of bar snacks? The fancy ones."

Nate scratched behind his ear. "Um. Maybe?"

"He did. I was there," Abi said as she stood, having been crouched by one of the fridges.

Nate opened his mouth, glaring at her. "Well, there you go then. Guess he did."

Abi chuckled. "I wouldn't bother tryin' to get any sense out of Nate today," she said to Pops. "He's been in a world of his own since I got here."

Nate side-eyed Abi. "Traitor," he uttered. He didn't

want to discuss what was going on in his head, and certainly not with Pops.

"So," Pops folded his arms on top of one of the boxes he'd put on the bar, "what is it? Maybe we can help." He lifted a finger, pointing between himself and Abi.

Nate shook his head. "It's nothing, honestly." Since the night Jared had kissed him, his head had been a mess. It didn't matter whether he talked to anybody else or not, in the end it was a decision he had to make, and eventually, he had. When Jared showed up at the bar, he knew if he wanted to keep on spending time with him, he had to take a step.

A step? It had felt like a whole damn leap. But he'd done it, he'd asked Jared out.

And now what?

"Nothing, huh. Try saying that again, maybe this time you'll sound like you mean it." Pops grinned.

Nate sighed. "Where do people go to eat?"

"Is this a trick question?" Pops raised an eyebrow and glanced over to Abi.

Abi threw up her hand. "Oh, oh, I know. Pick me."

"I mean, what kind of food. If you were taking someone out to eat. Where would you take them?" Nate tried to be vague but was pretty sure he just came across as talking nonsense.

Pops stroked his bearded jaw. "I guess that depends on the someone."

"You mean a date," Abi stated.

Nate lowered his head and looked at Pops through his lashes. "It's not like that."

"Uh huh." Abi's eyes sparkled with excitement. "You've *so* got a date."

"You do?" Pops sounded surprised, but the smile on his face was gentle, warm. "Is this why you wanted me to cover for you on Saturday?"

"It's not a date. It's…" Nate kneaded his brow. "Yes, I have a date," he admitted. He had the overwhelming urge to apologize to Pops.

Pops nodded, and then patted the top of the box he was resting against. "Abi, I think I'll leave this one to you." He stood straight. "I'll finish restocking the fridges."

"Don," Nate said without thinking.

"Hey now. Don't go getting all serious on me. Way I see it, it's a good thing you're goin' on a date." Pops' eyes filled with emotion, a strange happy-sad in them. He cleared his throat. "It really is." He smiled. "But I'll leave this to the young folk." As he walked away he said, "Abi, good luck with this guy."

Abi saluted then turned to Nate. "Here to help, boss."

Nate's chest tightened. "Yeah, Thanks." *I think.*

"Is it that one from the other day?" she immediately asked when Pops was out of earshot, then proceeded to ask a string of questions. "Or someone else? Wait, is it a man? Or did you find yourself a nice lady friend? Where? Was it on one of those dating apps Gregg was trying to talk you into joining with him?"

Did she even stop to take a breath?

"Yes," he said and held her gaze.

"Yes? To which one?"

When he didn't clarify his answer, she sighed. "Fine. I'll shut up. Tell me what you need."

Nate pulled out his phone. "I don't know. But it's *yes* to the first one. My date's with Jared, the man who came to the bar last week."

She grinned, looking pleased with herself.

"What I need is some ideas. I haven't dated in… a long time and have no idea what I'm doing." He turned his cell over in his hand. "Rhea, she knew I was useless at this stuff. If she wasn't the one organizing things, she'd leave some very obvious hints lyin' around."

"The date, is it just dinner?" Abi suddenly sounded serious, though there was a soft tone to her voice.

"Yeah."

"Hand it over." She wiggled her fingers. "I have a couple of ideas."

"Really?" He unlocked his phone and handed it to her.

She flicked her thumb over the screen. "Yep. I would have had a few more but you'd struggle to get a reservation now for Saturday." She smiled. "Okay, how about this one." They bumped shoulders as she came close to show him. "Everyone loves Italian." She tapped the screen and the menu popped up. "I recommend the meatballs."

"Ricci's. Have you been there?"

Abi nodded. "My sister works there so I could maybe even get you a discount."

Nate glanced at the website. Italian food could work. He just hoped any lasagna they served wasn't of the crispy, burned variety.

"It's a pretty new place, kinda out of the way, but the food's good, nice atmosphere."

"Yeah?"

"Yeah, and I'm not just saying it because my sister works there." She laughed.

"Thanks." He smiled. "Really, thanks."

"You're welcome." She rubbed his shoulder. "I'll go give Pops a hand. The phone number is on the website." She tapped the top of his phone as she passed. "Need anything else, just let me know."

Nate inhaled. "Okay. No putting it off." He scrolled back to the restaurant's home page and jotted down the contact information to make the call.

A few minutes later, he'd reserved a table for two and was sending the details on to Jared.

Sounds great, Jared messaged back, and relief flooded Nate.

He'd taken another step in Jared's direction.

The next few days passed in a blur of work and Luka, and finally it was Saturday morning and the mission to secure Luka a new pair of shoes.

"Well, that was easier than I thought it was going to be." Nate glanced at Luka who was sucking on a lollipop.

No way had that been enough of a treat for Luka to stare willingly at walls of shoes.

"Are you sure they fit okay? You didn't just say that?"

Luka shook his head and swung the large paper bag

that contained the boxed shoes as he walked beside Nate.

"If you say so." Nate hugged Luka to his side as they swerved to avoid people coming from the opposite direction. "Is this because of the sleepover?" He looked down at Luka, whose lips twitched as he sucked his candy. "So that's why you were on your best behavior? I already said you could go."

Luka pulled the lollipop from his mouth with a wet *pop*. "We went into three shops. I tried on loads of shoes."

"No. It wasn't that many."

"Was, too." Luka's brow creased as he complained. "You're just being weird and forgetting."

Nate frowned. "Three?"

Luka nodded.

"Really?" Nate rubbed his chin. "Huh?" His gaze drifted over the store windows as they walked. With a sigh, he slowed to a stop and stared at a mannequin dressed in a black paisley shirt and skinny jeans. He hadn't even considered what he'd wear tonight for his date with Jared.

It's okay to be looking forward to dinner, isn't it?

"You're smiling again?" Luka pointed out.

"I am?"

"Yes."

"Sorry," he said with a chuckle.

"Why?"

"Why am I sorry?" Nate queried.

"No, why are you smiling? You keep doing it and not

listening to me and made me go into three shops." He
pouted.

"Okay, okay. I'm sorry. I'll make it up to you."

Luka narrowed his eyes.

"What?"

"Why?" he repeated, clearly referring to the way
Nate had been acting.

Nate turned to stare at the mannequin. He hadn't
told Luka he was seeing Jared that evening. He wanted
to figure out what, if anything, was going on between
him and Jared before telling Luka more. Luka seemed to
like Jared and Nate was sure he'd be excited to get to see
Jared again, but if things weren't going to work out
between them, then he didn't want to leave Luka
disappointed.

"Dad," Luka whined.

Was he being overly protective? "Fine."

Luka brightened instantly.

"I'm going out to dinner tonight… with Jared."

"That's great." Luka grabbed his hand. "Let's go."

"Go where?"

Luka pulled on his arm and walked toward the store
doors. "You always buy me new clothes when I go to a
party."

"It's dinner not a party."

Luka didn't seem to be listening and tugged
harder, the doors sliding open when they got close
enough.

Nate gave in and followed him inside.

"Let's find the one in the window."

"Let's find a price tag," Nate muttered to himself.

He watched Luka's back, the excitement radiating from him was infectious.

He's smiling, right?

Nate's heart swelled. After all, that was all he wanted —Luka's smiles. He gripped Luka's hand, his cheeks twitching as he felt a rush of emotion. His own smiles didn't feel so bad either.

Luka bounced from foot to foot as he waited for Pops by the apartment door.

"Have you got everything?" Nate folded his arms and leaned back against the door jamb.

"Yes. Yes," Luka said.

Nate shook his head. "Did you eat more candy?"

"No."

"What's got you so excited? You have stayed over at a friend's house before, you know?"

Luka nodded. "But it's been forever."

"With good reason," Nate pointed out.

Luka curled down the corners of his mouth. "I said I was sorry and wouldn't do it again. And I haven't."

"I know. And that's why you're allowed a sleepover."

"Maybe you and Jared could have a sleepover, too," Luka said innocently.

"It's just dinner."

"Then next time I could stay at Auntie Lee's and he could use my bed."

Nate pursed his lips. "He could I guess." He was relieved when the intercom buzzed. "That'll be your grandpa." He lifted the receiver. "Come on up." He buzzed Pops into the building. "Are you sure you have everything?" he asked Luka.

Luka opened the door and stuck his head out into the corridor. "Yep." He stood there and waited until Pops made it upstairs. "He's here." He went to dash outside, but Nate caught him by the hood of his sweater.

"Hold up, kiddo."

Pops appeared in the doorway. "Hi," he said and quirked an eyebrow as he watched Luka duck and twist under Nate's arm, and ended up with his hood wrapped around his face.

"Don't ask," Nate said and released Luka who dropped to his knees with a grumble.

"Wasn't gonna." Pops chuckled.

"Thanks for taking him to his sleepover," Nate said.

"No worries. Was over this way anyway because of covering for you. Might as well drop this fella at his friend's while I'm at it."

Nate nodded. "You've been a big help."

"You know you can always ask. Even adults need to go out to play sometimes. Isn't that right, Luka?"

Luka stared up at them from where he had remained sitting on the floor. He clearly hadn't been listening as he pulled a face before saying, "Yes."

"Yes, what?" Nate met Luka's eyes.

"Um, yes, please?"

Nate laughed and Pops sighed. "You're both useless, the pair of ya. Come on, let's get out of the way so your dad can get ready for his date."

"It's not a—" Why was he trying to deny it again? Was it for Pops' benefit? For Luka's? Or for his own? A way to keep his expectations low, to keep some distance between him and Jared? He was still scared to get attached to someone new.

I want to keep moving forward. The steps he'd taken… They couldn't be for nothing.

"Thanks," he said instead.

"Dad's got a date," Luka said. He chuckled, acting cute and embarrassed at the word *date*.

Nate reached down and pulled up Luka's hood. "Both of you," he looked at Pops, "just go already."

"Make sure you wear it!" Luka said as he scrambled to his feet. He stood at Pops' side. "Dad bought a new shirt. I picked it for him."

"You did?" Pops smiled and glanced at Nate. "If you chose it, I'm sure Jared will love it."

Luka grinned then jumped back toward Nate to wrap his arms around his waist in a hug. "Love you," he said. "Have a good date." There it was again, the cuteness, the childish smile and the puffing of his cheeks.

"See you tomorrow." Nate followed them through the doorway. "Thanks again for tonight," he said to Pops.

"Sure."

"Bye." Nate gave a small wave and watched Luka walk alongside Pops to the stairs.

And now I'm alone. Again.

Nate pushed the door shut and stood for a moment. A date. He was going on a date. Why was the reality of his situation only hitting him now? And why did he feel as if he was back in high school, his first date, all fumbling and unsure of himself?

"It'll be fine," he said on a long, exhaled breath. He pulled out his cell. There were no notifications. Everything was going as planned, right?

He sent a quick message to confirm he and Jared were still meeting at the station and heading to the restaurant together.

Yep. All good my end. See you in an hour, Jared wrote back.

An hour.

Their date was in an hour.

I need to get ready.

Chapter Thirteen

Something was different tonight. Jared had expected a quiet dinner where he'd get to know Nate better, maybe talk about the bar—and when they'd met at the station he'd seemed nervous, and Jared had to think that he just wasn't ready to date again.

So in the space of the ten minutes they were on the train heading for dinner, Jared had worked it all through from Nate being a future lover to friend, and even though he had to fight the instinct to get another kiss, he was mostly happy with that. Nate had seen a lot, he was a responsible dad, he had bills to pay and a bar to run, and Jared could be a very good friend—people just had to ask Ethan.

But, by the time they'd reached the restaurant it was as if Nate was having some kind of similar internal conversation, only his upshot was that he'd given himself permission to relax and have fun. Over spaghetti, he opened up and told a hundred interwoven stories that revolved around Luka and the bar, and sometimes the stories overlapped. Jared could've watched him talk all night, note the way his eyes lit up when he was close to the end of a joke, or the pride that made him smile when he spoke about Luka.

Nate had a really beautiful smile, and there was no way Jared could handle being *just* friends. Friends didn't want to back their friend into a wall and kiss them forever.

Waxing poetic now.

"Do I have something…?" Nate pressed the napkin to his face and went cross-eyed trying to check himself out.

"No."

"It's just you were staring, is all, and…"

Jared took Nate's hand, lacing their fingers behind the jar on the table containing the mix of pasta that formed a display of sorts. No one would see them holding hands, not that it worried Jared, but Nate might not have wanted to even hold hands, let alone in a public place.

Only Nate didn't pull his hand back, instead he squeezed Jared's fingers and then carried on talking about the time that Gregg and Luka made a cocktail that was orange juice mixed with lightly smashed oranges, with a twist of orange.

"He was only six, and he brought it into the office for me, so proud that he'd made his first cocktail then he ran back out and fetched a napkin as he'd seen Gregg and me do."

"Was it a nice cocktail?"

"It was very orangey, with a hint of citrusy orange."

"Was it missing anything?" Jared encouraged Nate to continue with the joke, just so he could see Nate grin and then laugh.

"Orange?" Nate smirked as the waitress came over and removed their plates, leaving menus for dessert.

"Do you want anything?" Jared asked as he flipped to the dessert page with one hand, definitely not letting go of Nate. Well, not until they had to pay and leave, and then maybe there would be a chance to link hands again as they walked.

"I've never been here before, but Abi said they do this tiramisu cheesecake that's really worth the calories." He glanced at Jared. "Not that you have to worry about that," he murmured, and then dipped his gaze, focusing on the menu.

"Nor do you," Jared responded.

There was a moment when Nate worried the spoon in his hand as if he was making some monumental decision, but Jared didn't get to hear it because the waitress was back. He opened his mouth to order dessert, but Nate beat him to it.

"Is it just me who wants to go home and…"

Did he mean go home and end the night or go home and *whatever*. When Nate squeezed his hand again Jared considered it was the *whatever* that was winning for them both.

"I want to."

Decision made; Nate took charge for a moment. "We'd just like the check."

The waitress nodded and was clearly trying hard to hide a knowing smile. "Any coffees?" she asked.

"We can get coffee at mine," Nate turned to say that to Jared, and Jared's libido perked up at the heat in Nate's eyes. "If you like," he added after a moment.

"Just the check, then," Jared agreed, and thank god she appeared to understand where this was going because she fetched the check and brought the card machine with her. A few taps later and they were out on the sidewalk, bundled into coats and staring at each other in the light of the streetlamp.

"So you really want to come back for coffee, and by that I mean, kissing?" Nate asked hopefully. There was a boyish innocence to the man that captivated Jared, and then there was the heat in his eyes and the way he reached for Jared's hand and gripped tight.

"Yes."

"Just like that?"

"Uh huh."

Nate tugged Jared to a waiting cab. "I'm not wasting time on a train," he announced.

Jared climbed in after him, buckling up as Nate gave his address. "I like your thinking."

They laced hands again in the backseat, sitting in a silence that Jared didn't want to break because he didn't want to spook Nate. They made it from the taxi to the front door without touching, and then when they were inside they didn't jump each other, because this was going to be super civilized. With all of Nate's worries and concerns, Jared sensed he had to tread with care.

"Nate—oomph!"

Nate was on him in an instant, stealing his thoughts with a heated, desperate kiss, and pressing Jared to the wall, hard and needy against him. This wasn't a man considering what to do next, or deliberating with thought and worry, this was all about sex and lust, and Jared went from zero to sixty in a heartbeat.

"Off," Nate demanded, and Jared could get on with that as Nate wrestled with their coats, and shirts, and unbuckling jeans, Jared getting in on the act as soon as he came to his senses. They kissed as they ripped off clothes, backed from the wall and down the hall to the bedroom Jared had half seen last weekend. "You need to be completely naked." He shoved Jared toward the bed, then at the last minute caught him in a heated kiss, as if he couldn't decide what he wanted to do.

Jared pushed his jeans down with one hand, toed off his shoes, even walked back a little to slip his socks off and then, nude, the two of them separated.

"It's been a while—" Nate began, and Jared kissed away the doubt as they tumbled back onto the bed together, and landed in a tangled heap, hard against each other. "I don't want to disappoint you."

Jared kept kissing him, rolling them so he had the upper hand, groaning when they slotted together as if they were meant to be this close. He slid slowly, his cock bumping Nate's, and watched every moment of Nate's reaction and his soft whimper as he closed his eyes and arched up into Jared's hold. If they weren't careful Jared was going to lose it way too fast, and he wanted this to last. He slid half off, Nate chasing for the kiss, and Jared ignoring him, tracking kisses from his lips to his throat and then sucking marks on his skin, focusing on his nipples as Nate writhed under him. Then it was Nate's turn to flip them, and fuck it was hot when he manhandled Jared and held his hands over his head. They kissed for the longest time, Nate pressing himself lazily to Jared, then backing off, his breathing heavy.

"It's been forever," he muttered against Jared's throat, then kissed from throat to hip bone before coming back for more drugging kisses. "Oh, God…"

They set a rhythm, rocking, so close, and the kisses exchanged heated breaths and tangling tongues, and then Nate warning he was close, and he was going to end this if they weren't careful.

"Do you… can I …" He pulled away, lying on his back, and Jared got his first good look at Nate's cock, the perfect size, wanting his mouth there. Nate stopped him with a hand to his chest before tracing down to Jared's cock and wrapping his hand around his erection. "I have condoms," he sounded almost shy, and then kissed Jared. "Will you fuck me?"

Jesus. "Holy…" Jared was running out of superlatives, then when Nate reached for condoms and lube it seemed as if the entire room shrunk in on them and it was all too real. "Are you sure that—"

Nate stopped the question with a kiss, then widened his legs and reached between them, lube dripping from his hand, cursing when he couldn't get the right angle. Jared was there in an instant, swiping his fingers through the lube and pushing inside Nate, a little bit, but enough so Nate would feel him. Nate pushed down against the touch, then moaned and closed his eyes, arching his neck, and Jared withdrew his fingers and suited up before he got covered in lube and lost focus to the slippery mess. Then he went back to work, stretching, kissing, catching Nate's hand until they were both pressing inside, and then in a smooth action Nate moved to all fours.

"Now," he ordered.

Jared had never seen anything so hot, changing position fast so he was there, pushing gently until he was seated deep inside Nate, and then he couldn't move, because if he pressed any deeper he was going to lose it in an instant.

"Please…" Nate murmured, and Jared began to move, reaching around to get his hands on Nate's beautiful cock. The rhythm he set was slow, certain, strong, and all too soon he was close and then Nate stiffened and groaned. "I'm… fuck…"

Jared's orgasm came as Nate clamped down on him, when the wet heat of Nate's cum coated his hand.

They both collapsed back onto the mattress, panting, blissed-out.

Or is that just me?

"Holy shit," Nate muttered and then rolled on his side to kiss close to Jared's sensitive nipples, but then he traveled up and captured another kiss. "That was…"

"Yeah…"

"I needed that more than you'll ever know," he admitted.

"Happy to oblige," Jared offered, his sixth sense with these things sensing that Nate was withdrawing, maybe even regretting. "It was fun," he tried for light and easy, and eventually he managed to kiss a smile back on Nate's face.

Keep it simple. Don't push him.

"We have to do that again," Nate stated and laughed into a beautiful promise of a kiss, which Jared knew he would remember forever, even if this was the one sole time they ever got to do this.

They kissed lazily, explored each other, breaking apart when Jared knew he really had to leave. He might have fucked up one too many jobs for Bryant & Waites, but tomorrow was a commitment, and as much as he wanted to stay wrapped in Nate's arms, he had to make a move. They kissed as Jared dressed, when they made it to the door, and when they said goodbye.

"Call me?" Jared asked.

"Yep."

"I'll call you."

Another kiss.

"We can call each other."

"We can do that."

One last kiss, then Nate cradled Jared's face. "You're beautiful."

Another kiss. Just one, and then Jared *really* had to go. "So are you."

"I wish you didn't have to go." Nate smiled into yet another final kiss.

And then there was no way to avoid the fact that he had to leave. He walked backward down the hall like a lovesick teenager, sketched a small wave and then he turned his back on everything they'd done and headed home. He made it all the way to the sidewalk, heading left before his phone rang—Nate.

"Hey, you," Jared murmured.

"This is me calling. Just to say night."

"I'll let you know when I get home."

Neither of them ended the call. Jared encouraged Nate as they talked about everything and nothing, both wrapped up in the sensory hangover of what they'd done, until at last Jared was at his door.

"I'm home and now I need to go," Jared said.

"Jared?"

"Yeah?"

"I'm falling for you; I should warn you about that."

Jared smiled into the night and pressed the numbers to get into his building.

"Too late, I'm already falling for you, too. Night."

"Night, Jared."

Chapter Fourteen

Nate stood in front of the bookcase. His gaze was fixed on the photograph from his and Rhea's wedding day. He thumbed the back of his wedding band.

It had been almost a week since he'd slept with Jared. The sex had been hot, satisfying. But that wasn't all his time with Jared had been. They'd had a date, talked, connected, held hands across the table. The urge to get closer had built from there and sex had happened. Sure, it might have scratched an itch, but it was an itch Jared had started. He'd wanted to be with Jared because it was him.

It *had* to be him.

He glanced at his ring. He thought he would wear it forever, but if he had a chance at something new, something different... A new relationship, a new love. Could there finally be a reason to remove it?

Getting ahead of yourself.

They had been on one date.

We should probably make it to two before I start throwing around love.

"If that's okay with you?" he said to Rhea's image. She was smiling, and it almost felt as if that smile was from right then, real and warm and giving him permission.

Maybe I'm going crazy.

"Dad!"

Nate looked over his shoulder when Luka came running into the front room. His eyes were wide, and he held the cordless phone in one hand and performed a peculiar interpretive dance while waving his other arm around. "What is it?"

"Can I go?"

"Go where?"

"To the movies with Keegan?" He shoved the phone in Nate's direction.

"Sure, when?"

"Now. His mom will come get me."

Nate opened his mouth. "Right now? Okay, but"— Luka darted out of the room—"remember I'm working tonight so you'll need to go to Lee's when you get back," he called after him.

"Dad said yes," Luka said loudly. "Okay. Bye."

Nate sighed, following after him. Luka rushed about his room, opened his drawers and closet, pulling out clothes, adding to the already scattered toys and books and belongings on the floor.

"Luka," Nate chided. "I thought I asked you to clean up, not make more mess."

"I'll tidy it," he insisted. "I want to wear my Pac-Man Tee."

Nate glanced over the piles of clothes. "Here." He bent down and pulled the black T-shirt from among some others.

Luka grinned. "Thanks, Dad."

"No problem. Now, before Keegan's mom gets here, pick the stuff you want me to drop at Lee's for tonight, okay?"

Luka nodded. "Okay."

Fifteen minutes later and Luka was heading out the door. "Here," Nate said and handed him some bills. "But not too many snacks, got it?"

With a nod, Luka huddled with Keegan, the boys laughing together.

"He's staying at my neighbor's tonight because of work. You have her number still? Just in case."

"I do." Keegan's mother smiled. She was a tall woman with long, straight black hair and heavy bangs set against her pale skin. She had the appearance of a porcelain doll, but appearances were deceptive, she was anything but a fragile doll. "Come on you pair," she said in a brisk tone. "You want to have time to get popcorn and sodas before the movie starts, don't you?" She walked away.

"Yes, Mom," Keegan said and stood straight, gripping Luka by the wrist and dragging him along as they followed her.

"Bye," Nate called after them.

He shut the door, considered what to do with his time before heading to the bar. First, he needed to take

Luka's things over to Lee's. He made his way to Luka's room and surveyed the chaos. Luka was a kid and made kid-mess, but this was on a whole new level.

"Oh, Luka," he grumbled and started picking up the clothes Luka had thrown about. Luka had been asking for his room to be decorated for the last month. There needed to be a serious decluttering before that happened.

Carefully, Nate folded the clean T-shirts and put them in the dresser, piled some of the books Luka had left lying around, and generally tidied around, then picked up the backpack Luka had set aside. He hadn't realized the zipper was open and cursed as the contents in the top of the bag fell on his foot. He pressed his lips in a line and wiggled his toes, and with a sigh, bent down, tucked Luka's journal back in his bag and collected the loose sheets of paper that had scattered across the floor.

What's this?

Beneath one of the pages was what looked like a business card.

"Bryant and Waites," he read, having picked it up. "Who are they? Attorneys?" He turned the card over. It was a simple design—all black and gold and angled lines. Apart from the company name the only other detail was a phone number. He stared at the digits. Why did Luka have something like this?

He tapped the card on the back of his hand, considered what to do. Was this something Luka had picked up or had someone approached him and handed it to him? Why?

Screw it. Before his mind crafted some bizarre scenario, he should just call the number on the card. He pulled out his cell, typed in the digits and waited.

"Hello. Bryant and Waites, boyfriend hire service. This is Rowan speaking; how can I help?"

Nate quickly hung up. "Boyfriend hire," he uttered. He eyed the card. What kind of *hire*? Escorts? Was it that kind of thing? Not that it mattered, he was more concerned with how Luka had gotten hold of their business card. His first instinct was to head straight to the cinema, wrap Luka in a hug and insist they talk— what in god's name had Luka gotten hold of? Panic gripped him along with the idea of calling the cops and sickening thoughts of who had been around his son, but then he counted down from ten and pulled himself together. No point in panicking yet.

I need to talk to Luka.

He glanced at Luka's journal. He had promised himself, and Luka, to never pry, to give Luka his own space for his thoughts and feelings, but finding the card wasn't sitting right with Nate. The journal's lock was just for show and with a squeeze of the clasp it opened.

I'll just skim through for any mention of this Bryant-Waites place. Nate felt bad but he wanted to be sure. As far as he knew Luka hadn't been acting any differently, and if he had, he was nearly a teenager so acting differently and teen years went hand-in-hand. Apart from taking off by himself the other week, everything had been the same as normal.

He started at the end of the journal, flicked back through the pages. He didn't read every word as he scanned for any mention of the company. Jared's name appeared in some of the newer entries, but Nate didn't read further. When or if he and Jared looked to become a real, lasting relationship, then he would talk to Luka.

"Oh," he said out loud then read from the page he'd stopped at, "Dear Mr. or Mrs. Bryant and Waites, my Auntie Lee said that you let people borrow boyfriends…" Nate raised an eyebrow. "Lee, what on earth have you been telling him?" He continued, "… and I want one for my dad. It's his birthday… a nice present…"

It's your birthday soon. I wanted to get you something.

"Luka. Don't tell me…"

Your son was near my work.

Nate closed the journal, slipped it back inside Luka's bag and closed the zipper.

He hesitated for a moment, then redialed the number.

"Hello. Bryant and Waites. This is Rowan speaking; how can I help you?"

"Hi, sorry to bother you but I was wondering if Jared was in today?"

"He isn't I'm afraid. Is there something I can help you with? Do you have a reference number from a booking or—"

"No, no reference number."

"Oh, okay. So, is this for a new hire? If so, you'll need to send us through your requirements, location, dates etcetera. Is it Jared in particular you're after? Did he work with you on a previous occasion?"

"Actually," Nate massaged his brow, "I'm sorry, something's just come up, but thank you for your help."

"Oh, sure. Not a problem. We look forward to hearing from you."

"Yeah." He ended the call, then stared at the phone for the longest time. Had Jared been hired? And with what money? And what was Jared out there doing? And how could that affect Luka? He pulled up his contacts to make another call.

"Hey, you," Jared answered after a couple of rings.

"Am I disturbing you?" Nate asked.

Jared made a strained sound, as if he was stretching. "Nope. I was just reading the same page in a textbook for the tenth time."

Nate picked up the business card, tapped it on his chin. "Can I see you tonight? I think we need to talk."

"Is everything okay?"

Was it? Nate didn't know what to say or think, but he let his rational side do the talking. "Yeah, just some stuff came up. Come to the bar when you can."

"I'm nearly done here, meet you soon?"

"I'll be there."

When Nate hung up he stared at the phone some more, as if it could give him all the answers. He didn't want this to be an issue, he liked Jared a lot—more than a lot maybe—and he didn't want this to be fake. *What have I gotten myself into?* He groaned and scrubbed at his eyes. "Luka, what did you do?"

. . .

"Your beer," Nate said with a smile, and handed Jared his drink.

"Thanks." Jared brushed the back of Nate's hand as he took the bottle.

Nate caught Gregg's eye. "I'm just going to take a quick break. I'll be in the office if you need me." He indicated to Jared to follow him through to the back.

"So, we're back where the magic happens," Jared said as he stepped inside.

"Something like that," Nate said with a laugh and closed the door behind them. He stood for a moment and observed Jared who seemed relaxed in the small space.

"I was happy when you said you wanted to see me. Not that your texts hadn't made me happy, but seeing you again..." He sipped his beer. "I really enjoyed dinner last week."

"Me, too," Nate said.

Jared placed his drink on the desk, then came to stand in front of Nate. "Can I kiss you?"

Even though he wanted to talk, it was suddenly imperative that he got one last innocent kiss. Just to remind him if he was on his own again.

Nate nodded. He closed his eyes as Jared cupped his face with one hand as he kissed him. Jared ran his other hand over Nate's hip, teasing his fingers beneath the bottom of his shirt and brushing the skin of Nate's stomach.

A shiver ran up Nate's spine and the chill made way for a heat that immediately headed south. "Wait," he said and pulled back.

Jared gently stroked his thumb over Nate's cheek. "What's wrong?"

"You're serious about this, us, right?" Nate reached into the back pocket of his pants.

"Yes."

"You remember how I said I was falling for you. I want to be able to fall, but I need to be sure."

"Of course I'm serious about you. Why wouldn't I be—" He looked down when Nate brought up his hand and pressed it, along with the business card to his chest.

"So, that job of yours?" Nate said. "I'd love to hear more about it."

Jared's eyes widened. "Where did you get that?"

"It doesn't matter where I got it. I just need for you to explain to me what *this* is." He held up the card. "What is it you do, Jared?"

"It's sorta complicated."

Nate shook his head. "It doesn't have to be. I called the number on the back. A boyfriend hire service I think whoever answered said."

"That would be Rowan."

"I don't think that really matters right now. Is this place a... Are you a..."

"Am I what?"

"Are you an escort?" Nate rubbed the back of his neck. "Look, I'm not judging you, I mean, I'm sure it's a great job and as long as you're being safe when you're *with* people then you're an adult so... It's just... Luka. I have to think about Luka and what's best for him. I know it should be about me and you, and maybe if it was just us I could handle what you do, but it's not. Luka is a thing and always will be. I mean, you're a student and I guess the money must be good." He met Jared's eyes. "You weren't made to do it, were you? You haven't got piles of debts have you?"

Jared shook his head. "Nobody's making me do anything."

"Right. So, you really are…"

"Wait. That's not what I meant. I'm not an escort." Nate leaned back when Jared gripped his shoulders. "I'm what we call a *boyfriend*. One you can hire. A companion available for weddings, parties, events. They can hire me for a day or a week or whatever, within reason."

"So, not an escort?"

"No. No, definitely not. I'm not saying others might not have, you know, and I'm certainly not saying I haven't been propositioned, but that is not the role I'm hired to do. I'm simply there to help people. Be it for support maybe while attending a wedding, or so someone can show an ex how they've moved on, or just simply being a friend and spending time with them. I guess being a psychology student I found the people who used such a service interesting."

"Okay."

"Okay? Okay, what?"

"Just, okay. I don't know what else to say."

Jared gripped him more tightly. "Then what do you need to hear? I meant what I said. I am serious about us and I didn't mean to lie, well, I didn't *lie*-lie. I didn't think it mattered, not in the beginning."

"Are you sure about that? Isn't it that you didn't say anything because of Luka?"

"I don't—"

"Dear Mr. or Mrs. Bryant and Waites." Nate sighed. "From the look on your face, I'm guessing you've heard the rest. It's where he was when you found him, wasn't it?"

Jared admitted, "Yes. He came to the offices."

"We must have seemed pathetic to you."

"Why? He just wanted you to be happy and he thought this was a way you could be."

"Is that why you stuck around?"

"No," Jared said, and Nate believed him.

"I don't imagine his pocket money comes anywhere close to what it would cost to really hire you."

"He sure tried." Jared stepped back and pulled some money from his pants' pocket. "Each time I saw him, he pushed these at me. I was keeping hold of them until I could give them back to him. Because I swear, although in the beginning I wanted to help a kid desperate to make his dad happy, being near you, hanging out with you, and Luka, in the end I kind of forgot about all that. I wanted to know you because you're you and the more I did the more of you I wanted to see."

"I think you saw plenty last week." Nate lowered his head, embarrassed.

"So, what happens now?"

"I wonder," Nate said. His feelings for Jared were real, and from what he could tell, Jared's were too. Those hadn't changed in the last few hours, and he didn't see why they should. His real issue was with Luka.

He'd made his own son worry about him. He'd have to have a serious conversation with him tomorrow. Maybe even have Jared there. They could both talk to him, explain he didn't need to worry, and Jared didn't need to have loose change thrust at him every time Luka saw him.

"I'll tell you on one condition." Nate decided.

"Anything." There was an unexpected thrill to seeing Jared act so desperately.

"Kiss me." He moved closer. He smoothed Jared's collar.

"Is that it?" Jared swallowed hard.

"What? Were you expecting me to punish you? I'm not really into that."

Jared smiled. "Am I forgiven?"

Nate tilted his head, kissed Jared's cheek. "Nothing to forgive. But no more weird secrets with my son."

"So just normal ones?"

Nate sighed and pinched Jared's nipple through his shirt.

"Ow, ow. I give up."

"Well, what are you waiting for? Kiss me."

And Jared did. The kiss was firm, full of desire and relief.

What both felt for the other, was real. Nate was sure of that.

I want us both to fall completely.

Chapter Fifteen

The chat with Luka went well. Considering.

Nate organized a movie night with popcorn, and before they started eating he told Jared and Luka to sit on the sofa and took his place on the stool facing them.

It felt to Jared a bit like an interrogation, and it was clear that Luka had decided something was up.

"What did we do?" he asked, then leaned into Jared. "Dad only ever sits there when I'm in trouble."

"You're not in trouble," Nate started with a patient tone.

"Feels like it," Luka muttered.

"Agreed," Jared said out of the corner of his mouth, and Nate's lips twitched with the hint of a smile.

"Well, I wanted to talk to you both about Bryant & Waites."

"Uh oh," Luka said.

"Uh oh," Jared repeated.

"Luka, I know you think I've been lonely, and you're

right, I have been. Only buying me a date is probably not the way to go about it."

"How did you even find out?" Luka was wide-eyed.

"He's got powers," Jared fake-whispered to Luka.

"I know!" Luka whispered back.

Nate's smile twitched again. "Never mind how I found out. Now, Jared, I want you to give Luka his money back."

Jared rooted in his pocket and pulled out the handful of coins, offering them to Luka palm up. Luka refused to even look at the money, and in a dramatic move he sat on his hands.

"But I don't want the money, I want Jared to stay, because when you see him you're smiling more, and you even whistled this morning. Please let him stay, Dad, please don't let him go. I promise to do all my homework."

"Luka…" Nate sounded anguished.

Jared leapt in to defuse the emotional time bomb. "I'm not going anywhere, buddy," he said, and placed the coins on the table. "I'm staying for free." He then hugged Luka and pressed a kiss to the top of his head. "Your dad wants me to stay."

"I do."

That called for a group hug, and the hugs lasted a very long time.

Movie night ended with Luka falling asleep sprawled over the two of them, and it was Jared who ended up carrying him to bed. Luka woke once, startled, staring up at Jared, and then relaxing. "He's staying," he murmured to his pillow, and then curled on his side.

Jared's chest tightened. "Love this kid," he whispered in the dark, and searched for Nate's hand, tugging him in to steal the tiniest of kisses. *Love his dad, too.*

"I wish you could stay tonight," Nate said after they shut Luka's door.

"The car is picking me up at five for the booking."

"What is it this time? Man, woman?"

Jared was still hung up on the personal revelation that he was falling in love with Nate. "Huh?"

"Did a man or a woman book you?"

"Businesswoman, I've worked for her before, she's fascinating."

"Have fun."

"I will, the food is always excellent, and they are a... oh." He finally got a good look at Nate's expression, which was closed and just this side of worried. "I'd rather be staying the night here, then waking up to you, then eating pancakes and watching TV with Luka."

"Yeah?"

Jared did all he could to kiss the worries away. "It's just a job. I'll come straight back on Sunday and tell you all about it."

"Maybe you could... nah, it's okay."

"Maybe I could what?"

"I don't know... you could call me when you're away? Because I'll be missing your face, and I think I already miss your voice. Only if you want."

Oh yeah, I'm well on the way to being in love.

· · ·

"And then everything went to shit." Jared paused for a moment and shook his head. He was listing the latest series of disasters on his Bryant & Waites booking and he loved that Nate was so invested.

Nate chuckled and the sound sent shivers down Jared's spine. He'd missed Nate's voice as well, and was so lost in the sexy timbre of it, and the way he laughed, and the sense memory of how he hugged, and the sex…

Yeah, the sex was hot. Off the charts hot. Addictive even.

"You have to tell me everything," Nate said, and Jared heard him moving, the sound of the refrigerator opening and shutting, then an exhalation as he sat on the sofa. Jared could imagine Nate doing all these things, and knew every single expression, and the steps he would take.

Not that he'd been staring at Nate every moment he got. *Liar.*

Today's Bryant & Waites booking had started off so well. Jared had chosen the perfect suit, a crisp white shirt, a ruby-red tie, and after the appropriate amount of primping and messing about in the bathroom he looked good if he said so himself. Even Nate agreed after Jared had sent him a whole raft of photos.

"I was holding my own, discussing the psychology of sales with these execs, and my date gave a rousing speech about how ninety-nine percent wasn't a hundred, or something like that. I'm not exactly sure what she said because I was thinking about you the whole time."

"You were?" Why did Nate sound so surprised? They were dating officially, and even though their time alone had been tight what with Jared's studying, the bar, and dates where Luka was with them, they'd already had some amazing moments.

"Are you telling me you don't think about me?" Jared deadpanned, which made Nate laugh again.

"Wasn't it me who asked *you* to call?"

"True that. Anyway, if you're really interested in how it all went to shit, then Jeanette finished her keynote, and I was mingling."

"Uh oh."

"Why uh oh?"

"Mingling sounds ominous."

"To be fair mingling is pretty innocent and it didn't start in any kind of ominous way, but then I met Carl with his cat Marmalade."

"You've got to be kidding me. One of the execs actually took their cat to the event?"

"No, it was more like, Marmalade had just had results back from tests for blah blah blah, something, blah, and was fine. Carl got upset is all, and I stood with him while he worked the emotions through his system, y'know."

"So far so good."

"Oh, did Luka get my text about the dinosaur thing? The one at the museum?"

"Yes he did. Stop changing the subject."

"Only there's this guided tour and we——"

"Jared…"

"Well, both of us leaning on the same temporary table probably wasn't a good idea, but it wasn't as if we knew the table would break. But it did, and that meant that me, Jeanette, and Carl were close to the chocolate fountain when it lost its equilibrium, which ended up with all three of us wrestling in the slippery chocolate." He paused to allow Nate to finish laughing. "I think it should be a thing."

"What? You and strangers wrestling in chocolate?"

"No, *you* and me wrestling in chocolate."

"Oh."

"Exactly, and now I've thought of that, I'm all hard while being completely on my own in this gorgeous room."

"Hang on, because I'm taking this into the bedroom," Nate murmured.

"Well, I took Jeanette to our suite, and tucked her in, and she had a good cry about wanting a real boyfriend, and I gave her some advice. She wasn't going back down, so I locked myself in my room and there was chocolate everywhere."

"Where, everywhere?"

Jared settled back on the pillows, ignoring his damp post-shower hair and imagined Nate doing the same in the bedroom that Jared had grown to love. It was all pale blues and dark wood, and *so Nate*, and the memory of what they'd done in that bed just made him harder.

"It soaked through gaps in my shirt, all over my chest, my nipples." How was it that such an innocent word, said in a darkened room, with a lover at the other end of the phone, could sound so erotic? Jared heard Nate moan low in his throat, and lust flooded him until he had his hand curved around his cock and in an embarrassingly short amount of time, to the sounds of Nate getting himself off, Jared's orgasm hit him like a freight train, leaving him panting and breathless.

"I'm ordering us chocolate body paint," Nate muttered. "Just as soon as I can move."

"Nate?"

"Hmmm?" Nate sounded as if he was settling in for the night, and Jared imagined him pulling the covers over himself, rolling onto his side just the same as Jared was.

I love you. I wish I was there with you so I could kiss you goodnight, because you're all I can think of, and I know you're not looking for another dad for Luka, but I love him as well, and I'm just consumed by it all.

"Goodnight," Jared said, letting instead everything bubble up inside him. What he wanted to say needed to be said face to face, with added kissing. It wasn't something he should be offering up after phone sex.

Getting to tell Nate that he loved him was taking Jared far too long. At first it was exams that stole his time, then when they did meet up they had Luka with them. He loved being with Nate and Luka, and today's visit to The American Museum of Natural History was one of the best days he'd ever had. Only, there hadn't been a single chance to tell Nate what he felt, at least not in the way he wanted to do it, which was going to be something romantic. Over dinner maybe. Or in bed.

For sure it shouldn't be something they talked about under the ass end of a woolly mammoth.

"I bet the poos they did were huuuuge," Luka commented as he stared up at the enormous skeleton.

"Big enough to bury you," Jared teased, and then ruffled Luka's hair in an approximation of a quantity of mammoth poo landing on his head. Luka ducked away and darted over to the T-Rex, Nate and Jared following at a slower pace.

"Thank you for suggesting this," Nate said as they reached the information board for the dinosaur. He'd grown more relaxed as the day went on, as if just being out with Luka had lifted a weight from his shoulders. "I needed today."

Jared brushed his hand against Nate's but there was no expectation of holding hands—after all not everyone was as fond of PDAs as Jared was. Only, Nate curled his hand into Jared's and laced their fingers, and they read the board.

"Sometimes I wonder if it's all worth it," Nate blurted.

Jared realized Nate wasn't looking at the board at all, but up at the skeleton. Jared was good at making connections but the evidence at hand, Nate staring up at a T-Rex and making a sweeping statement, wasn't making sense. "What?" *Us? Are you thinking because now we held hands, that we're not worth it?*

"The bar, working so hard for so little, when I could be..." He pressed fingers to his temple.

"What else would you like to do?"

"It isn't that." He turned a little to face Jared. "Nothing else. I love the bar, I just don't want the rest of it, and that's not right is it? Nothing worth having is easy, but when I think…" he lowered his voice, but Luka was a long way from them in the fossil display. "… losing Rhea, and not being there for Luka, and I'm so happy with you, and I think of all the things that I want to do, and then there's this big weight."

Jared tugged him over to the bench, and sat them down, right where they could keep an eye on Luka.

"Maybe you need to make a change," he offered after a short pause.

Nate side-eyed him. "I won't sell the bar."

"I didn't mean you should, but you have Pops in covering shifts, so what if you give Gregg more responsibility, maybe even let him buy into the place?"

"No, it's our place. Anyway, Rhea's dad would…"

"What? You think he'd be disappointed, angry, sad? You should talk to him. But first of all, Nate?"

"Yeah?" He was distracted by Luka calling them, but he did turn back to Jared with a soft smile.

This was the moment, in the quiet corner of the museum, right in the middle of the best day. "I love you."

Surprise stole Nate's smile, and then his eyes widened. "I love you, too."

"Dad! They have a snail and it's bigger than a car!"

They didn't get the chance to talk any more about life decisions, or love, but they held hands the entire museum visit, and Nate couldn't stop smiling.

Jared called that a win.

Chapter Sixteen

"Well, this feels kinda awkward." Gregg sat in the chair beside Nate's and scratched the back of his neck. He wore a crooked smile. "I'm half-expecting a scolding." He eyed Nate. "So, what is it? Calling me in before opening, must be serious."

"You've worked here, at Rhea's, for what? Six years."

"Nearly seven," Gregg said with a nod.

"And you're thirty?"

"Nearly thirty-one." Gregg grinned.

Nate sat forward. "I wanted to talk to you about this place and maybe making a few changes to running it." Jared had sown a seed last week, and he finally felt ready to act on the idea.

Gregg sucked on his teeth. "What kind of changes?"

"Okay." Nate clasped his hands together. "Obviously, this will all depend on what plans you might have for the future, but I was wondering if you'd like to run this place, for real."

"In what way?"

"Basically, you'd be the manager, run things out front. So, more hours, more money. We could discuss a new assistant manager."

"You can afford to do that?"

"I've crunched the numbers. It'd work."

"And that would mean what for you?"

"I'd be more behind the scenes, the business side. At least for now, until Luka is older. Despite having this place, I've always done everything I could to be there for him. I can't say it's been easy, and I've had people help me a lot, you included, but I guess what I'm getting at is I need to be better where Luka is concerned. In the future... I don't know, but I feel like..." He paused. "I used this place to bury my head. It was an excuse to ignore a lot of things..." He waved his hand in front of his chest. "Things in here and I don't want to hide, close myself off anymore. I want to take the chance that's presented itself to me."

"Jared?"

Nate lowered his head.

There was a brief silence, then Gregg said, "Okay."

"Really?"

Gregg nodded. "I mean, you asked me so nicely." He smiled. "Honestly, I hadn't thought much about the future. I'm comfortable here." He exhaled through his nose. "Maybe if Rhea was still around, she'd have bullied me out of here and forced me towards bigger things before now, but I like it here. The staff, the customers, the atmosphere." He shrugged. "And as you said, the future, who knows, but for now, I'm up for it."

Nate's thoughts went to Rhea. "She really would have, wouldn't she?" He couldn't help but smile. "Anyway, we'll work out the details over the next week and get it down in writing soon. Is that okay? Anything you want to know?"

"One thing."

"Sure."

"Is it okay if I make a suggestion about a new assistant manager?"

Nate leaned his head to one side and listened.

"I'd like to put Abi's name forward. She's been pretty dependable recently and it seems she's been thinking of looking for something with more hours and money, so I think she'd be interested. That okay?"

"That's fine, and I agree, she's been a great help."

The conversation changed from business to idle nonsense, and eventually Gregg excused himself.

It was as if a weight had been lifted from Nate's shoulders and the rest of the day flew by, until the last hour to closing.

"I want to go home," Nate mumbled as he lurked near the bar.

Abi joined him. "Have you got something good waiting for you? Or is it someone?"

Nate folded his arms across his chest. "Neither. He's meeting me here."

"It's creepy."

"What is?"

She waved her hand in the direction of his face. "Seeing you all smiley."

"Is it really that weird?" He was going to end up getting a complex over it at this rate.

"It's not that you're smiling, but just the…" She raised her shoulders. "I don't know. They've more oomph than they used to have and there's more of them. Not that I didn't appreciate your serious brooding face. You know it was all like…" She narrowed her eyes and pouted. "I'm Batman," she said in a husky voice.

"You done?"

"Yeah, I'm done." She stood straight. "Oh, customer," she said, excusing herself in a series of bouncy side-steps.

The minutes counted down slower than Nate thought possible, but at long last they reached closing time.

"Goodnight," Abi said as Nate locked up.

"Night." Nate watched her walk down the street to her waiting boyfriend, then checked his phone. Jared had texted to say he had been held up. Something about his roommate and how he'd explain later but was now on his way to the bar.

"I could have met you somewhere else." He sighed and rested against the shutter.

"Nate."

Nate stood and gave a short wave. "Hey."

"Sorry. Were you waiting long?"

"Forever."

Jared's face dropped. "Really?"

"No, not really," Nate said with a smirk and took a step. "We've only just locked up. Promise."

Jared pressed his hand to his chest in relief and joined Nate as he walked.

"Is everything okay with your roommate?" Nate asked. "We could have just met up in the morning."

"No, no. I wanted to see you, and yeah, Ethan is fine. Well, as fine as Ethan ever is. I don't really know how he does it, but I'm starting to think he's a beacon for assholes. Every single man he's dated ends up screwing him over somehow."

"Maybe he should hire himself one. A nice guy like you," Nate said.

Jared smiled. "A nice guy, huh?"

"Mmm. Very nice." Nate nudged his shoulder to Jared's as they walked. The backs of their hands brushed together, and Nate let out a contented sigh when Jared caught hold of his fingers. They walked hand-in-hand to the station, a chaste kiss before boarding the train heading for home.

"Hey," Nate said in a hushed voice, laughing as Jared grabbed him and they stumbled together through the door and into the apartment.

"I missed you," Jared mumbled into Nate's back as he hugged him from behind. "Did you miss me?"

Nate leaned his head back, pushing his cheek to Jared's when he rested his chin on Nate's shoulder. "Of course, I did." He closed his eyes as Jared moved his hands lower and rested them over his belt buckle. It'd only been a few days since he'd seen him last, but he loved having Jared around.

"Can we?" Jared whispered in his ear. "Luka's not here, right?" His lips brushed Nate's neck, his teeth grazing the skin slightly as he nudged Nate's earlobe with his nose.

"He's at his grandparents. All weekend."

"All weekend?" Jared asked.

"It'd be impossible to decorate Luka's room if he was here. He'd be in and out of there wanting to help or wanting to get something—a book, a sweater, his school bag. Easier this way, so…" He spun in Jared's arms and rested his palms on Jared's chest. "I can't have you distracting me too much. I, no, *we* will complete all tasks this weekend. Got it?"

Jared nodded. "I got it. But we're not starting *right* now, right?"

"No, but we do have to get up in the morning to go buy paint."

"It'll be fine. We'll get up." He pulled Nate close, his crotch pressing against Nate's thigh.

Nate sucked on his teeth. "Seems like somebody already is," he teased.

With a groan, Jared rested his forehead on Nate's shoulder. "Don't say things like that."

"To be young, huh?" Nate said and reached between them. He cupped the front of Jared's pants. "Okay, you have my attention, but you'll have to settle for a hand job. A quick one."

"Seriously?"

"If you'd prefer to go straight to sleep—"

Jared lifted his head. "No, quick is good."

Nate chuckled, gently tapping the back of his hand to Jared's bulge-strained pants. He met Jared's eyes. "Come on," he said and took hold of Jared's hand.

Time is precious.

"I love you." Jared held Nate's hand tightly, tugging him back and into an embrace. "I mean it."

Nate smiled, relaxing into Jared's hold. "I know you do." He stroked Jared's jaw and angled his head to meet him in a long, firm kiss.

And I intend to make the most of our time together.

They made their way to the bedroom in between kisses, laughter, and hugging and stripping away layers of clothing, until they came to lie together on the bed. They lay facing each other, each grasping the other's dick.

Nate nipped at Jared's bottom lip and gripped his erection, shifting his pace from long, firm strokes, to rougher, quick tugs.

Jared let out a throaty grunt.

"Oh." Nate turned his head, pressed his face into his pillow as heat rose in his gut, excited by the prolonged kissing and touching.

I want to come so bad.

Jared slid his free hand over Nate's hips, encouraging him closer before tracing his fingers backward and toward Nate's butt.

"Hey," Nate uttered and bit at Jared's chin.

"What?" Jared grinned, slipped his hand lower and pressed between Nate's butt cheeks.

"You don't play fair," Nate said.

"All's fair in love and…" Jared kissed Nate. "Something, something."

Nate clenched his ass. "Behave." He thrust his hand down, his fist bumping Jared's swollen balls.

"Ah," Jared groaned. He dug his fingers into the flesh of Nate's ass as he thrust into Nate's hand. "Fuck."

"Together," Nate said, smashing his mouth to Jared's, hungry kisses, panting, overwhelming sounds and sensations as they brought each other to a climax. Jared first, Nate chasing his own orgasm a heavy heartbeat later.

"Fuck," Jared said again and rolled onto his back.

Huffing a breath, Nate sat up. He leaned over and kissed Jared. His heart was still racing. "Let's clean up and get some sleep," he said.

Jared caught hold of Nate's hand. "I love you."

Nate smiled. "Same."

"What's that?" Jared came to stand behind Nate in front of Luka's bedroom door.

"It's a surprise." He pressed the wrapped gift to his chest.

They'd spent the morning staring at various shades of green paint, then paintbrushes as the ones Nate had thought they were going to use were still covered in paint and hard as rock.

When was the last time I used them?

"Please?" Jared hugged him from behind.

"It's not for you," Nate said. "It's for Luka." He glanced down at the purple tissue paper wrapping. "And maybe a little bit for me."

Jared rested his chin on Nate's shoulder. "Are you okay?" His tone changed from teasing to soothing. "You're not regretting us, right?"

Nate raised his arm and stroked the back of Jared's hair. "Don't make me have to repeat myself. I'm a grown man making grown-up decisions. I want to be with you. Maybe all these years I was waiting for you somehow." He leaned his head to Jared's. "I'm too realistic to believe in things like fate, but, just maybe, Luka turning up at your office was a little bit of that."

Jared kissed his cheek.

"Anyway. This." He unwrapped the paper to reveal the wooden plaque.

"Luka," Jared read.

"It's to replace the one on his bedroom door." He touched the raised lettering. "He's always moving forward; he's growing up." He looked at Jared. "And I guess I need to do the same, well, the moving forward part." He held the sign up, covering the one that had been on Luka's door since he was a baby. "Time to move. Not exactly earth-shattering but for me, for you, it's a sign I'm ready. At least, to wrap up the old one with great care, and tuck it away in a box somewhere safe." He chuckled, his smile falling away as he turned his hand. "This, however, I'm not quite ready to take off," he said of his wedding band. "It's too final feeling for now at least."

"You don't have to ever take it off if you don't want to." Jared wrapped his hand around Nate's.

Nate shook his head. "No. That's sweet of you to say, but no, one day, when I'm ready, it'll come off. I just need a bit longer, you know?" He faced Jared. "Is that okay?"

Jared hugged him. "As long as you need."

"Thanks." Nate closed his eyes and rested his head on Jared's chest. He listened to the beat of Jared's heart, such a comforting sound.

One day, not too far from now, I'll be ready.

"I love you," he uttered.

And I'll fill my heart up with you.

Epilogue

"Luka, dinner," Nate called from the kitchen.

"Coming," he yelled, his feet thundering along the corridor as he rushed to the dining table.

"Did you wash your hands?" Nate asked.

"Yes." He looked at Jared. "Did you?"

Jared laughed. "Yes, cheeky." He pulled Luka's chair out, resting his arm on the back when Luka sat down.

"What is it?" Luka asked when Nate put a plate in front of him.

"You really are being cheeky tonight."

Nate handed Jared a plate. He smirked as if he was going to ask the same question. "Chicken noodle casserole," Nate said and sat down.

"Nana Kay makes it all the time." Luka picked up his fork and started eating. "Hers is nicer."

"It's exactly the same," Nate insisted.

Luka shrugged.

"I used her recipe."

A grin spread across Luka's face.

"Are you messing with me?" Nate sighed. "Whatever. I like it."

"Me, too," Jared said before filling his mouth. He smiled with puffed cheeks at Luka.

It'd become a new normal for Nate and Luka. Jared joined them for dinner every couple of nights, or more often if work and school allowed. It had been that way for three months. For the first time in years, it wasn't just him and Luka around the dinner table.

Between the bites of food, conversation was easy, relaxed. They talked about things that made the others smile, laugh, want to hear more. It was really beginning to feel as if they were a little family, the three of them together.

"I have something I want to show you," Nate said after dinner. Luka was in his room reading, having left Nate and Jared to clean up.

"Is it something sexy?" Jared swayed his shoulders.

Nate laughed. "No." He took Jared by the hand and led him through to the living room. "I bought something but thought you should do the honors." They stopped beside the bookcase.

"And do what exactly?" Jared eyed the shelves.

Nate picked up the slim box he'd placed beside the bookcase earlier. "Don't get too excited. It's just a…" He shook his head. "I don't know what it is, but here." He gave the box to Jared and waited.

Jared tipped the box. "A photo frame," Jared said. He turned it over to see the photograph. "This is from—"

"The museum the other month. Luka wanted a

selfie of us all and well, I thought…" He carefully made space, parting some of the other pictures on the shelf. "I thought it was time for some new pictures. New *family* pictures." He bit his lip.

"Are you sure?" Jared gripped the frame in both hands. "Because this is…" He smiled. "Because I love it."

Nate nodded. He meant it. "The family I, Rhea, and Luka made, that's its own thing, it'll always be there, but I think the three of us can be happy, so if you're okay with us, then, I'd like this to be the first picture of many *many* more. Our new family."

"I really do love it. Thank you." He kissed Nate's cheek, then turned back to the shelf, placing the photograph in the space Nate had made.

"Happy?" Nate asked.

"Are you?" Jared met his eyes.

Nate glanced at the collection of photos. He smiled, turned to Jared. "Yes." He pressed his hand to Jared's face. "I didn't think I'd ever be happy again. In some ways, I didn't want to be happy. But you've given me something new to smile about. *You* make me smile, make me happy." He leaned in for a kiss. "Thank you, Jared."

"Anytime," Jared said, kissing him again.

An *eww* came from behind them, followed by fake vomiting sounds.

Nate turned to find Luka standing in the doorway. "How long have you been there?"

"Since now." Luka shrugged.

Clearing his throat, Jared backed away.

"Oh cool. The picture from the museum." Luka

jumped toward the bookcase. "That mammoth was awesome."

Nate stood behind him, rested his hands on his shoulders. "It *was* pretty awesome."

"Can we go again? Or maybe somewhere else?" He turned his head. "Jared, too."

"Of course, me too," Jared said. "We'll go somewhere when we're all free, okay?"

"Cool." Luka jumped on the spot, then spun around. "Bathroom," he said then scurried away.

Jared looked at Nate and they laughed together.

What a funny thing his new little family was.

And I love it, and them. Luka and Jared, both.

Read Felix and Ethan's story – coming soon

Sign up for a release reminder: rjscott.co.uk/rjnews

Felix (Boyfriend for Hire 4)

Felix

Ethan is determined to face the ghosts of his past when he attends his high school reunion. Hiring a boyfriend as a pretend date seemed like a sensible idea on paper, but sexy Felix is everything Ethan wants in a man for real.

When Ethan hires Felix, it's just another job. But, after a single night together, Felix finds himself imagining an impossible future with the cute science nerd.

Their attraction is off the charts, but when real life gets in the way, love might become impossible to keep a secret.

Sapphire Cay

Sapphire Cay

1. <u>Follow the Sun</u>
2. <u>Under the Sun</u>
3. <u>Chase The Sun</u>
4. <u>Christmas In The Sun</u>
5. <u>Capture The Sun</u>
6. <u>Forever In The Sun</u>

Also from RJ & Meredith

Standalone Christmas

- The Road to Frosty Hollow

Free Reads

- Stronger Together

Meet RJ Scott

RJ discovered romance in books at a very young age and realized that if there wasn't romance on the page, she could create it in her head. With over one hundred and fifty books published, she is a full time author of gay romance.

She lives and works out of her home in the beautiful English countryside, spends her spare time reading, watching films, and enjoying time with her family.

The last time she had a week's break from writing she didn't like it one little bit and has yet to meet a box of chocolates she couldn't defeat.

www.rjscott.co.uk | rj@rjscott.co.uk

NEWSLETTER - rjscott.co.uk/rjnews

facebook.com/author.rjscott

instagram.com/rjscott_author

amazon.com/author/rj-scott

bookbub.com/authors/rj-scott

goodreads.com/rjscott

patreon.com/RJScott

Meet Meredith Russell

Meredith Russell lives in the heart of England. An avid fan of many story genres, she enjoys nothing less than a happy ending. She believes in heroes and romance and strives to reflect this in her writing. Sharing her imagination and passion for stories and characters is a dream Meredith is excited to turn into reality.

www.meredithrussell.co.uk
meredithrussell666@gmail.com

facebook.com/meredithrussellauthor
x.com/MeredithRAuthor
instagram.com/miss_meredith_r